MAGGIE'S TURN

Joan Bird

www.**BOROUGHSPUBLISHINGGROUP**.com

MAGGIE'S TURN
Copyright © 2024 Joan Bird

ISBN 978-1-957295-84-8

To Larry, my soulmate, best friend, and husband.

Thank you for proving forever lasting love exists, and not only on the

pages of a book.

ACKNOWLEDGMENTS

As always gigantic thanks to my publisher and editor for never failing to encourage, nudge, and help shape a better tale.

Also, gratitude to Boroughs' copy editors, grammar gurus, and gracious correctors of continuity issues. You know, like a blue-eyed heroine in one scene having tears spill from brown eyes three chapters later.

Kudos to all the people I've encountered in life, without whom I'd have no resources to build the characters for my stories.

Finally, a quick and special thanks for support from Terry Carmer, a long-ago roommate/friend who despite enduring great loss in the last few years, embraces life and laughs at my jokes.

MAGGIE'S TURN

CHAPTER ONE

Nick a.k.a. "Coop"

Nick's daughter stared at him, and he bit back a smile. Purposely, he ignored his child, who was hovering at the edge of his desk, knowing whatever she was about to tell him was a bad idea for any number of reasons. He knew the folly of it, since avoiding her questions for the last two years had been a failure. In the end, not responding only served to escalate her pop-gun inquiries. She was relentless.

"I'm writing, Noodle." He didn't put down his pen.

"Editing."

"Smarty pants."

"And Daddy, I'm not a noodle."

Nick still didn't look up as he scribbled another note at the edge of the printed manuscript. Technology be damned, he edited final drafts with pen and/or pencil on the printed page and probably always would.

"Ahem."

"Emily."

"Daddy."

He looked up then, struggling against outright laughter. Bedhead didn't come close to describing the disaster of blonde curls smashed flat on one side of her face. On the other side, matted wads of the same curls rested against one cheek puckered from sleeping on her coverlet.

There were fingerprints in the middle of both her eyeglass lenses, the purple frames accentuating round blue eyes that studied him intently. One hand gripped a baggie filled with cereal puffs. She was halfway through her seventh year, and the snack choice seemed in conflict with her too-sharp intellect.

"I have a plan."

Nick raised an eyebrow. "About?"

"Christmas, of course."

"Of course. You're aware it's only the middle of September."

"Daddy, I'm seven and a half. I *know* when Christmas is. But Mom always said we have to plan ahead." Coming from his daughter, the mention of Meg Cooper, especially in such a matter-of-fact way, felt like a knife being thrust into his gut.

"I apologize. Of course you do."

"Good. Now you need to listen."

Giving in, he shrugged, turned in his desk chair, and focused on his daughter.

Emily was squinting as if visualizing Christmas morning. She'd abandoned the cereal and, with her right elbow propped in her left hand, was tapping her index finger against her cheek.

"We need a party," she said.

"Oh, we do, do we?"

"Absolutely."

"Uh. No, we don't." He shifted his gaze back to the work on his desk, knowing it wouldn't stop his daughter from discussing her idea to its every last detail.

"Daddy, you need to give me a reason."

"I'm the adult, Em. What I say goes." With a sigh, he noted her eyes clouding with threatening tears. *Dammit.* Nick knew by not conceding, he'd have to deal with his daughter's predictable reaction. It wasn't that she was spoiled. She wasn't. But she missed her mother. And God alone knew that he understood that feeling better than Emily could ever understand.

The ever-present wave of emotions hit him and felt as if he'd chugged a mouthful of a slushie, causing a horrible brain freeze. Although he could manage the pain much better now, it was all too easy to be swept back into the well of darkness that swallowed him whole when Meg died. And, like now, when he saw the loss reflected in his only child, it weakened the walls he'd built to survive.

"You remember, Em?" He meant to distract her from her idea, which, if it took hold, would drive him nuts for the next few months.

"Remember what?"

"I have a parent-teacher conference in two hours." He paused, wracking his brain for the first-grade teacher's name. He took a chance. "Ms. Bennington."

"Mrs. Benning, Dad." He never knew why she'd switch from calling him Daddy to Dad or back. However, early on, he'd determined that Dad was the more serious of the two.

"You're right. Thank you."

"She likes me."

He almost laughed. "I imagine she does."

"I'm good in school."

"You are, which means, Em, you're capable of understanding my 'no' to a Christmas party."

He could almost see the wheels turning in her head. There was a good chance he'd cave as early as November. Then he'd be helping Emily plan a party for her friends, which would include Christmas cookies, ice cream, candy, and presents.

He smiled, remembering her fifth birthday. Meg had planned it all. But that didn't stop Emily from having veto power on certain things related to the event.

She'd walked into his home office in their old apartment, her hands on her hips, and said, "No clowns, Dad." Her hair was shorter then, so it bounced instead of flipping when she turned and marched out of his office. He remembered his response to the comment as she followed the rules and closed the door behind her: "Well, okay, then."

He shook off the memory with the realization Emily was staring at him with her ultra-serious face.

"And no fake Santa," she said. "I mean, everybody knows the real Santa's too busy to be walking around in stores or going to parties that time of year. Also, it won't be a party only for *my friends*, Dad."

He'd begun tapping his pen on the manuscript. "Like whom, daughter mine? I don't really have friends, you know that."

"Yes, you do, Daddy."

He tried his sternest look, with silence as an accompaniment.

She looked down at her toes, forcing him to shift his gaze and do the same. Ten colors of toenail polish. He might have to chat with their babysitter, Ginny. Except she was great, and besides, she was leaving. Her coursework at Columbia was increasing as she'd declared her major.

Ginny had become like family and would be hard to replace, which was why he should take Liz Callahan's advice and hire the woman she'd recommended for babysitting.

Weird, Ginny had lived across the hall from him in the last building. The old apartment. The Meg and Nick apartment. He swallowed hard and closed his eyes.

His dear friend Liz—he did have some friends, he supposed—had suggested he enlist his new neighbor, who also lived across the hall, as a babysitter. God, he missed his wife.

Emily moved closer, and he felt her small fingers tapping the top of his left arm. "Daddy?"

"Yes, baby."

"I know you're thinking about Mommy."

"I am." *Christ almighty.* How could he still be so unable to handle it? The memories, the loss. He had Emily to take care of—not the other way around. But here she was, being seven but acting forty.

He opened his eyes. She was staring right at him, intent, and a telltale glisten brimmed in the corner of her eyelids. "I miss her too." There was no hesitation. He swept her up and hugged her, burying a soft sob in her curls.

She smelled like apple shampoo and cereal, like life itself.

"Not so tight, Daddy," she mumbled into his shoulder.

He brushed her curls away from her face. "I'm sorry, it's just…"

"Hard to talk about Mommy." Laying her head against his shoulder, he noticed how she folded her hands together in her lap. So very Meg. As she rubbed away any evidence of tears with her balled fists, a smile replaced her transitory misery. "So?"

A single question. His daughter had the same ability as his late wife: she was capable of getting an answer to the question that had been put forth and argued during the last five minutes.

God, Meg. Are you really going to haunt me every moment through Em? There was no answer, no ghost of Meg to help him through this journey. "A Christmas party?"

"Yes, Daddy." She giggled.

"And you think I'm going to cave to your demands?"

She giggled again, and the damn dimples made an appearance on both sides of her mouth. "Yes, Daddy." No laughter this time. She was serious.

"Emily…" The first ring of the landline interrupted him. Lifting her off his lap, he stood to answer. Only a few close friends and business associates ever used the house phone, so he knew it could be important. "About a party: maybe. That's maybe in all caps, kiddo." He turned away, guessing Emily was leaping around behind him, fist-punching the air.

"I'm going to get dressed, Daddy."

Nick figured she'd turned down the hall to her room to make good on the statement.

He reached the small antique desk that housed pens, pencils, index cards, and a functioning answering machine. His laptop's home was in the large top drawer, its sleek modern design a contrast to the disarray atop the piece of furniture Meg had adored.

Shaking the memory of his wife laughing at his distaste for efficient writing tools and apps that corrected—in his view, overcorrected—the written word, he picked up the phone receiver.

"Nick Cooper here."

***

Liz Callahan Willis listened to the phone ring on the other end of the line. She wouldn't be surprised if Coop didn't pick up. Composing a message in her head, she waited for the answering machine. Old fashioned, or as he liked to say, "old school." Liz was aware he begrudged his cell phone with the force of a thousand curses.

It'd been almost two years since he'd lost Meg. Twenty-one months in which her friend, and Jake's best editor, had gone from wounded, heartbroken, and angry to recognizing the need to grab his daughter, hold on, and heal together.

And he had.

It'd also been four years since she managed her annual Christmas tradition of successful matchmaking. She'd purposefully held back on any effort to connect two lonely souls because she was focused on her best friend Maggie—whose life turned trainwreck—had taken those same four years to untangle. And the other small hitch? Liz needed the right hero for the project.

Nick Cooper, Coop to his good friends, was the answer to that dilemma.

When Meg died, Liz had thought of Maggie, but of course, Coop needed time, and Mags? Well, she was still unraveling the nightmare that had been her marriage.

Liz had never taken her set-ups lightly. That was part of the hiatus. But now everything fit perfectly. Liz was determined to gently push her bestest best friend toward a safe, happy, loving relationship.

Neither Coop nor Maggie knew it yet. That was part of the magic.

Liz's subtle efforts at bringing Coop from loneliness into a happy-ever-after with the Cinderella she viewed as an obvious soulmate had begun already.

A large apartment in Maggie's building had opened up, and it dawned on Liz: ta-da—the perfect set-up. How could she have missed it? Coop and Emily needed a change from the place they'd lived with Meg. The place where Meg died. So why shouldn't Liz share with Coop, the information that just such a unit had come onto the market? Coop had jumped at the chance to move. That it happened to be across the hall from Maggie? Perfect Kismet for moving Liz's planned matchmaking forward.

Step one of Mission: Matchmaking set-up accomplished.

Step two: Christmas was less than a hundred days away, so Liz had to get a move on. She listened to another ring, knowing that at least if he wasn't in, Coop's machine would take a message and act as a foot in the door to her plan.

"Nick Cooper here."

"Coop, I'm so glad I caught you." Liz grinned to herself.

Time to make the match.

CHAPTER TWO

Maggie

Mid-September

Maggie was curious about her new neighbors. Whoever they were, they'd moved in three weeks ago. Prior to that, the apartment had been unoccupied for at least two months, with frequent potential buyers coming and going to view the place while it was empty.

Perhaps there'd been an affordability issue for the three-bedroom, two-and-a-half bathrooms with a large outdoor deck, she mused. An apartment like that one should've been snapped up in an instant.

What niggled most, though, were the movers delivering big boxes labeled "Toys" and "Stuffed Animals."

She figured a couple with children had moved into the unit. But after that, she'd been too distracted with her own life to take up further covert surveillance through her peephole.

She'd been in her place for over a year, and she still worried about safety. Not the building or the area. Any concerns were specific to her.

There'd been three moves before her current residence, each taking her further away from her past. She figured it was like sobriety. Each move equaled a sobriety memento chip and was one more step away from the nightmare of her life with Ricky Amato.

He'd altered her destiny in a way that was worse than what'd happened years before, when her parents had died in a grisly car crash. Maggie and her younger brother had gone to live with an aunt.

When the trucking company responsible for the wreck settled, a generous trust fund was created for the siblings.

It'd paid for college.

And Maggie had done lots and lots of college.

Meeting her best friend, Liz "Lizzie" Callahan, was sheer luck. Liz had answered Maggie's *Roommate Wanted* note tacked to a bulletin board in the NYU Student Union. The two of them had begun finishing each other's sentences during their first meeting. She was counting the years on her fingers when a horn blasted from the street below pulling Maggie out of her reverie. Sometimes the habit of revisiting her past was crushing and time-consuming, which was why she'd spent the last two weeks getting the physical evidence of her living nightmare organized for storage.

Thankfully, all that was left to do was haul the two bankers boxes of documents down to the small storage space she owned in the basement. Out of sight, out of mind. She'd just dragged one of the containers to the door when the doorbell buzzed. Startled, since she wasn't expecting company or a delivery, she swore under her breath, hating that she was still jumpy. She had Ricky to thank for that.

She stared through the peephole. No one was visible, which, given her history, was more than disconcerting. She waited another few moments and then turned to continue working on her project.

The buzzer rang again.

Annoyed, she returned to the door, yanked the slide lock, flipped the deadbolt, and, risking an ax murderer, yanked open the door with a loud "So. Not. Funny."

A young girl with a book of some sort clutched in her hands smiled up at Maggie.

CHAPTER THREE

Maggie Meets Emily Rose

A young girl stood there, ramrod straight with hair that might've been styled by a blender. The lovely child had fair skin, pink cheeks, and wide eyes peering through a pair of glasses that needed serious cleaning.

"I'm Emily Rose Cooper," Maggie's unexpected visitor said.

"Hello, I'm…"

"Miss Maggie Reynolds." Smiling. "See? It's here in our address book."

Maggie went straight to concerned. Not about the tiny interloper on her doorstep but because of the intrusion itself. One, she'd been reminded of her status—single at forty-one—and two, a child she'd never met, who should have no clue of who Maggie was, had personal information in an address book, the origins of its keeper, unknown. She couldn't help having hit seven on a ten-point angry scale, snapping, "Says who?"

"Oh, Mrs. W. She knows you, and she found us our apartment." Emily twisted at the waist, jutting her chin toward the other side of the hall. "It's how Daddy bought it so we could move in."

Mrs. W.? Willis? It was the only Mrs. W. Maggie knew. Following the motion, Maggie noticed the open door leading into her new neighbor's apartment. She could see coats on hooks to the right in the small foyer. She'd gone across the hall with a buyer's agent before, the looky-loo moment arranged by Maggie's best friend who'd been scouting out the place *for an old acquaintance.* At least, that was what Liz had said at the time.

"Lizzie," Maggie said, still staring absentmindedly at the open door across the hall.

"Yes, ma'am. Mrs. Willis. She says I can call her Mrs. W."

That explained Maggie's name in a total stranger's address book. "I'm sure she does. But please, I could do without the ma'am." She paused at the child's giggle. What was she, all of seven?

"I'm seven and a half. And I'm here because we're planning a Christmas party. I know it's only September now, but I like to plan."

Maggie was a grade school teacher, for cripes' sake. She had experience with children but none with overly articulate seven-year-olds.

Okay, it *was* true she'd been around Liz and her brood for over a decade, but this extensive experience did not include the actual *mommy-ing* bit. Not the same as teaching by a long shot. All that scary stuff, like Annie's appendicitis, or when they'd had to endure a battery of tests to determine whether baby Ned had something terribly wrong with him.

"Are you somewhere else?"

The question took Maggie out of her head and back to the mini adult at her door. "Where'd you learn that expression?" she asked.

"From me," a deep voice answered.

Maggie took a step back, and Emily turned and squealed. "Daddy."

"I'm sorry, ma'am," he said to Maggie.

He didn't offer a hand to shake, nor an introduction, and rather returned his focus to his child. It left her no opportunity to object to his use of address. He scowled as he asked, "And you, Emily Rose Cooper, how many rules did you break in the last five minutes?" He stared down at his child.

Measuring against her own height, Maggie figured him for six-two. His arms, at rest and unthreatening, were loose at his sides.

From social butterfly to little girl in an instant, Emily twisted back and forth at her waist, staring at her feet, the address book closed and clutched in both of her small hands. It seemed as if she and her father were in a kind of stand-off.

After a short silence during which Maggie was pretty sure she'd seen her new hunky neighbor bite back a smile, Emily put her right arm straight out and held her index, middle, and ring finger skyward.

"Three. We're agreed." Emily's father seemed to be waiting for something, and as it turned out, the child needed no prodding.

"I left the apartment without telling you," Emily said.

"That's one." He remained stern.

Maggie was thinking her neighbor might be an asshole or a child abuser, a tyrant even, or worse. She was about to inject herself into the exchange but noticed his right arm, elbow flexed, his hand bent at the wrist aimed in her direction: a pantomime of a stop sign.

Also impossible to miss was the twitch in his cheek, confirming Maggie's earlier notion that he was, indeed, fighting back a smile.

"I'm never supposed to leave the apartment alone," Emily continued.

"Two." He squatted, bringing them eye to eye. "And three?"

"We were going to meet the pretty lady that lives across the hall *together*." Emily turned her face away from her dad and flashed a toothy grin at Maggie. "Miss Maggie Reynolds."

It resonated like a confetti-worthy "ta-da."

Maggie snorted. She couldn't help it.

Her otherwise dreary day was completely uplifted by Emily's lack of compliance with her father's rules, which apparently occurred more frequently than not.

It hit Maggie, that the handsome tall man and his way-smart daughter had been discussing their new neighbor.

Me.

CHAPTER FOUR

"The" Meeting

Tall Dark and Handsome asked her to wait while he ushered the charming Emily back across the hall. He said he'd like to "chat" a bit about being neighbors. Maggie had all kinds of descriptive terms for him, but she didn't know his name, except that he would likely be Mr. Cooper, given his daughter's self-introduction.

Drop-dead-gorgeous Mr. Cooper. Even if she *knew* his first name, it would be presumptuous to use it. *Yep, a bit too presumptuous.*

Now she felt like a dolt. She looked down at her smartwatch and, because its technology held more information than the Apollo rockets, thought it should help her determine whether to continue waiting or go inside her apartment, slam the door, and disappear.

Seven minutes.

Seven minutes and forty seconds. She'd waited. Feeling foolish. Standing at her open door, counting the handful of flaws and chips on her threshold and the doorframe.

Why am I waiting? Because Emily Rose Cooper's father commanded her to.

Okay, it was a request, and it wasn't his fault she'd gone limp in her knees when he'd smiled and said, "Can you give me a minute, Miss Reynolds?"

Oh, sure, why not? Does it show that I've got nothing to do? No hot date?

Why hadn't she said, "Not now," or, "Sorry, I'm right in the middle of something"?

She glanced at the open door to the Cooper apartment and saw no broad-shoulder hunk headed her way.

Maggie had also given away her penchant for casual couture. Orange running shorts and a faded red t-shirt that hung loosely on her not-so-curvy frame with orange and yellow letters representing her only half-marathon—and with a hole near the hemline from getting caught on a drawer handle in the kitchen.

At least he could still read the shirt's charity moniker, and possibly enough for the GQ dad to believe she'd been a serious runner at one point in her life.

She looked down and shook her head. "Damn it." She'd answered the door in her koala bear slippers. It should count she'd made a large donation to some save-the-bears foundation, but it didn't. She looked ridiculous. A good cause, sure, but not the best attire to impress her too-handsome-for-his-own-good neighbor.

She glanced back at her watch. Nine minutes.

"I'm sorry it took so long." The deep voice cut into her thoughts.

For the third time that morning, Maggie jumped. "Oh, no biggie."

"C'mon, Ms. Reynolds. You have rules too, right? My making you wait? Rude."

Maggie wondered if he answered all of his own questions. It didn't matter since she couldn't respond with a super-clever comeback because the air in her lungs had taken a hike.

She took a quick glance at his features. He was slightly grey at the temples, and his features were perfectly symmetric.

She gulped. His eyes had subtle hints of grey, but the primary color was blue. She wasn't sure because his pupils were dilated due to the dim light in the hall. Then he looked away, back to the open door of his apartment, and yelled, "You okay in there, Em?"

Maggie heard the muffled reply. "Fine, Daddy." He leveled his gaze on Maggie again, and his eyes took on a deep grey color, reminding her of rolling thunderheads. Fitting, because there seemed to be a storm brewing within him.

Like he was at war with something. Maybe even with himself, or perhaps he was in pain.

"Again, I'm sorry you had to wait. Even more so because Emily barged in on you."

"I suppose raising a seven-year-old comes with challenges?"

"You can say that again."

She almost did. It was in her nature to be a little snarky, more often than not, especially when intimidated. But she waited, wondering just what his reason was for still standing in the hallway.

"Oh, before I forget." He pulled an envelope from his back pocket. "This letter was delivered to our apartment, I guess by mistake. I've asked around; nobody wants to claim it. It's not addressed to you, but you're the only person on the floor I haven't checked with, so…"

She took the envelope from his hand and glanced at it. "Mrs. M. Amato" was scribbled on the front. Not typed. She looked at the back and then turned to the front again. There was no return address but a name printed as "T. Amato." It robbed her of breath, but she didn't dare reveal her emotions to her new neighbor.

She transferred the note to her left hand, reaching out her right to shake his. "I learned that Emily knows who I am, but in case *you* didn't know, I'm Maggie—"

He took her hand. "Reynolds. Yes, I know, we have a mutual friend in Liz Willis." His touch, though no more than a formal handshake, sent a warm sensation up her arm. "Cooper. Nick Cooper."

"Uhm…" As much as his handshake had warmed her from the inside out, the letter in her other hand made her feel like ice had taken over her veins. At the same time, her heart was banging against her ribcage.

She reined in the terror and gathered her wits. "Mr. Cooper." She disengaged from the handshake. "Let's talk about maybe getting together another day. Liz has my number—in fact, I believe you have it, and I need to go." Maggie turned on her heel so fast she nearly fell while slamming the door in his face so hard the sound reverberated throughout her apartment.

"Dammit, dammit, dammit." She crossed to her sofa and picked up a throw pillow, then punched it, thinking beating up something would help banish the fear the letter brought back to the surface. She started to crumple the envelope but knew doing so wouldn't solve anything.

"How the hell did he find me?"

The bankers box of her history with Ricky Amato sat where she'd put it down when she went to answer the door. It mocked her. That Maggie had actually believed she could box up all the evidence of the worst years of her life and move on... That was comedy, and the joke was on her.

She got up and went back to the door to peer out of the peephole. Nothing, and nobody, in the hallway. A chill raced through her, and she methodically activated all three locks on her door. She stared at the envelope again. All the return address divulged was "T. Amato."

Teddy. Ricky's brother. Maggie was the "M" before Amato on the envelope. For eight horrifying years, she had been Mrs. Maggie Amato.

For those eight years, she'd lived in a world that was ninety percent hell one hundred percent of the time.

She slumped onto the sofa and felt sick.

She stared at the box, knowing its contents by heart.

The court order changing her name back to Reynolds.

The state bar crap.

All the voluminous divorce papers finalized with no custody issues.

No children. Thanks to Ricky.

Maggie swiped at an automatic tear. A psychiatrist would probably tell her she'd taken up teaching because she felt guilty about losing the baby.

The painful memory never went away. But ultimately, she'd accepted it wasn't her fault. *Ricky*. He'd pushed her down the five stairs on the outside stoop of their apartment building.

That was when she'd called it quits.

So. She must've been insane to have agreed to show up at the one hearing after she'd turned him in and planned on turning state's evidence.

But in so doing, by Ricky's skewed code of ethics, her actions were unforgivable. Worse, the entire mess had landed her under the scrutiny of the legal ethics people, and so she'd thrown herself on the mercy of the Appellate Division of the state Supreme Court. Her attorney for the disciplinary action was brilliant and had convinced the committee she'd not been complicit in Ricky's illegal activities.

But, despite those facts, the court ruled that once she'd turned over evidence of his crimes, there were hints of impropriety, including actions rising to a level of moral turpitude. It was crap, and she knew it. At least they'd allowed her to resign from practice as opposed to facing disbarment—a distinction without a difference when it came to the reality of what she'd lost, but it meant something to her not to be completely humiliated.

Either way, her legal career was over.

Maggie didn't look back. She'd been healing physically and emotionally until six weeks ago when, while serving his sentence, Richard "Ricky" Antonio Amato was found murdered in a prison bathroom, a standard prison-made shank embedded in his liver.

It wasn't too long after that she'd started getting the phone calls.

And now? *The letter.*

She opened the one handed over from Nick Cooper.

A single newspaper page fell folded to the floor. Maggie picked it up. Though she'd read the article when it happened, the headline still glared at her:

Popular Local Musician, Ricky Amato, Found Stabbed to Death in Prison Bathroom.

The story went on to list all the details she already knew.

And why she'd received the ominous letter, she knew that too.

Teddy had found her.

The threat Teddy had made in the courthouse hallway after Ricky's sentencing was terrifying. He blamed her for ratting out Ricky, which resulted in his going to prison.

Teddy Amato had promised to find her and kill her. It wouldn't get any better now that Ricky was dead. No doubt Teddy blamed her for that too.

She bit her lip so deeply she tasted blood.

There'd been three phone calls, but she'd convinced herself they were pranks, especially since the voice was muffled, and it didn't sound like Teddy. She'd told no one. And she'd been kidding herself.

Now her GQ neighbor knew about this letter, but, thankfully, not its contents.

"Shit. Damn it. Double dammit. Eff you, Teddy."

His disguised voice rang all too clear in her head, invading her space and her very being. She'd moved three times since Ricky went to jail. Three times to three different types of places. All in New York City, but in different boroughs, hoping to make it harder to find her.

But he had.

The phone calls came in rough, poisonous tones. "I'm collecting for my brother, Maggie."

From what she knew about him, and by the venom in Teddy's voice, she'd probably be dead by Christmas.

***

Nick Cooper stared at the slammed door for a few seconds. He had the distinct feeling that the letter had been the impetus for Maggie Reynolds's abrupt dismissal. Hell, he'd kept her standing and waiting for almost ten minutes, and she had every right to be ticked off, but she hadn't been. So, logically, it had to be the letter addressed to "M. Amato." *M.? Maggie?* Yes, but Reynolds, not Amato.

Of course, Jake Willis, Nick's boss, could provide answers, but he figured it would be much more interesting, fun even, to get to Ms. Reynolds's secrets on his own.

CHAPTER FIVE

Jake

"You're at it again." Jake Willis pulled a swath of hair off his wife's face. She was resting against his chest. He wouldn't've disturbed their afterglow for anything other than a house fire, a sick kid, or, as now, a half-baked Lizzie-matchmaking scheme.

"At what?" Liz's voice was muffled as she snuggled closer. Her fingers traced his arm from bicep to wrist—usually a complete turn-on. Liz knew him well. She had an arsenal of ways to distract him when she didn't want to admit to something. Or, for that matter, discuss an issue they didn't agree on.

Too bad for his wife, he knew her even better.

"Don't try to distract me, Lizzie."

"I'm not."

"You are, and you know it. I figure you're plotting even now."

"What would I be plotting?" Before he could answer, she injected, "For your information, I was working on a story line."

"Liar. And a bad one at that. You're planning something, *and* it has to do with that thing that drives your writing and your happily-ever-afters. You're convinced everyone on Earth is entitled to forever bliss."

"Well, they are."

"Agreed. But that's not reality, tragic as it is, and you know that too."

He hadn't intended a reference to his first wife. Even if Liz took it that way, it never caused a rift between them. The deep breath in and out against his ribs confirmed she thought of Samantha for one second, maybe two, before moving on. "Listen Editor-in-Chief, I'm really thinking about my next book," Liz said.

"Yeah? And you'll probably base the plot loosely on another Christmas match-up."

She giggled against him; another turn-on. He adored everything about her. "Let's see, by my count, you haven't brought two people together for four years," he said. "I thought you'd retired."

"Hmph. That's *four* Christmas seasons." She raised her head and held up all fingers but her thumb. "Four. I mean, how tragic is that?"

Jake shifted quickly and rolled her beneath him. It wasn't her manipulating people's lives that made him crazy. Well, it did. But not *that* kind of crazy. No. For *that* kind of crazy, it started with her skin and the heat of her body. "You *are* scheming."

"Indeed."

"Indeed, my ass." He settled comfortably, letting her feel just how turned on he was. "All snappy comebacks aside, I heard you talking with Nick on the phone earlier."

Nick Cooper, Coop to his close friends, remained Jake's best editor at Willis & Bennett. He'd helped launch multiple bestsellers, and Jake appreciated Coop's talent.

"So?"

"So, you're up to your neck in some calculated meet-cute." Jake bent and kissed her forehead. "Don't bother denying it. You're planning Coop's next true love. And since I know you, he won't know what hit him."

"Honey. He's such a good friend, and he's alone."

"Not entirely alone. He has a daughter, and he's also my friend and my employee."

Her laugh came from deep inside her: a purr and growl combination. That too turned him on and flipped the final switch.

"Liz." He eased his flexed elbow and sank against her with a kiss. The kiss was telling. Deep and hot. He was fifty-five and thanked

God every day he could still make love to Liz. Maybe their crazy passion was the secret. Maybe he was just lucky.

His mind wandered for a moment to his life before Liz and didn't realize he'd broken their embrace until she started tapping behind his ears. "You fall asleep, old man?"

He laughed. "I'll show you 'old man.' And you have to watch what you say these days, *old girl*." He should've been prepared for her punch. After more than a decade of the damn things, he knew all too well her automatic reaction when they teased each other. "Ouch."

"That was mean. A woman can be sensitive about aging…"

He interrupted her. "When that woman's getting up in years—" This time, he chuckled at the punch, shifted his weight, and kissed her again. Their connection was hot. So hot that if someone kicked open the door and yelled "Fire," it wouldn't've stopped him from following where his visceral reaction was taking him. "Not mean, unless you think this is mean." He slipped inside her, watching the expression on her face.

"Jake." She sighed as she lifted her hips to meet his, tugging his hair, her words driving him as she moaned beneath him. As it always had been, their heat was intense, and neither of them had the discipline to slow the inevitable.

"There, Jake." Liz clutched his shoulders, her fingers digging into skin as she tensed every muscle in her body, cried out, then shivered beneath him.

He opened his eyes and held back his smug smile while taking in her obvious satisfaction. Then, covering her mouth with his, he muffled his own release in a consuming kiss and collapsed against her, his heart thundering against hers.

They lay, breathless and listening. The house remained quiet. No cries from a child with a nightmare. No tap on the door, accompanied by "Daddy, I need a drink of water." No sounds of a toilet flushing.

Liz shivered beneath him again, a quick spasm.

He knew she was but asked anyway, "You okay, sweetheart?"

"You're shitting me, right?"

"Ah, my girl's back. So lovely, so sexy, and so damned articulate." He grabbed her arms, pinning his wife in place before she could punch him again.

A shadow passed over her face.

"What's wrong?" he asked.

"Did you know I pray every day that we won't lose this loving thing we get to do?" Her eyes welled up, and a single drop escaped as a tear, sliding down one cheek. "The thought we won't *always* have this physical connection... It's stupid, but I get sad wondering when it will end. It's bound to happen someday. I mean, how will we know our last time will be our last time?"

"We probably won't."

"I'm being silly."

"A bit, yeah."

"And melancholy."

"A lot."

"It's so special. Do you think we'll manage this when we don't have teeth and my boobs are down to my knees?"

Jake barked out a laugh. "No teeth?" He kissed her brow, then her nose, finishing with a light kiss on her lips. "That could be interesting." He smiled at the light slap to his behind. Rolling off and to his side of their king-size bed, he tugged her back against his body and wrapped a strand of her hair around his index finger.

She sighed and relaxed against him. "Okay. I guess I'm over it. Now, where were we?"

"I was grilling you on a former dangerous Christmas habit of yours." The room was cool, so Jake paused to straighten the blankets and sheets around them. Fall was ushering itself in, and they both liked sleeping with the window cracked. "Which you circumvented by distracting me with your female wiles."

She turned and craned her neck. "Hey, you started it."

"I concede. Regardless, we were debating the wisdom of your matchmaking scheme."

"I never said I had a plan. I don't scheme."

"Well, I think you do."

"Okay. Like what? Where's your proof?"

"None yet. But how about your phone call with Coop earlier?" He stared down at her red tresses kinked from perspiration and smashed against pillows. "Are you denying you're going to try to set him up with someone?"

She took a deep breath, the action of which stirred him again. He put that on hold, sat against the headboard, and again reshuffled the sheets and blankets. Unless she wanted to suffocate under the covers, she'd be forced to sit up with him.

Punching her way free, she reached to the end of the bed, grabbed her robe, and slipped it on, settling herself on top of the covers. She sat, hands resting on her knees.

"What's this?" He motioned at her distance. "A line in the sand?" He tried to sound serious but knew he couldn't keep up the act. Grinning, he bit back further comment.

"Of course not. But you know I can't think straight if you're close enough to touch me. And you're sneaky. You men think women have all the wiles." She leaned across to her nightstand and grabbed a scrunchie.

The motion of tying wads of her hair into a pony tail momentarily freed one of her breasts from the robe. His lascivious grin got the intended reaction because she chastised him with, "This is serious stuff. Pay attention."

"I agree, this is serious. So please keep your tempting parts covered."

She offered him a big toothy smile and tightened her robe. "So, it's not really matchmaking."

"Go on."

"Well, you know Coop bought the apartment across from Maggie, and that makes it kismet."

"Maggie? Our Maggie?" He rubbed his cheek, scratching at late-night stubble. "And this kismet, however you came to the conclusion, gives you free rein to set them up?" He wouldn't admit it to Liz, but the fact that Coop had been a widower for almost two years and that Maggie and Coop were both a little lost was obvious. Still, the match she was proposing? They weren't ready for what she had in mind.

She was using the fingers on her right hand to count down the reasons she was right. "Meg's gone, and nothing can change that. But then there's Em. You know Maggie loves, loves, loves kids. And I figure Coop's a lot like you. An editor who's a sharp dresser and quite handsome." She drew the word handsome out, no doubt to tease him. "Plus, like us, he's older than Mags."

"Not *much* older."

"Right. By about three years. But Maggie and I are so much alike, and I think Coop has many of your qualities. It's destiny."

"Besides being an editor and *sort of* older? I'm not convinced."

"Like you, he's got a little grey in his hair, and he's also a teeny bit stuffy…"

"Hey." But he laughed. He couldn't help it when Liz was on a roll. "I'm assuming you find the ever-increasing grey is okay on me?"

"Oh, yeah. It's yummy. So distinguished. You're becoming a silver fox."

He grinned. "And what about the stuffy part?" He leaned forward and grabbed her left hand. It forced her to shift her position and steady herself, but she didn't move any closer.

She blew an errant strand of hair from her face. "Let me get this out."

"You think I'm uppity, like some kind of upper-crust snob?"

"No. That's not what I'm suggesting. Definitely not uppity. But Coop is, well, sort of standoffish. I guess that comes from losing Meg."

"Okay. I know I can't stop you, Lizzie, but I need you to promise me you'll be careful on this matchmaking thing. You've had a good run, but if this goes wrong, you're liable to have a broken-hearted mess on your hands, and neither of them have the emotional bandwidth to withstand getting battered."

This time, she didn't object when he took her hand. "You and Maggie *are* a lot alike. But that doesn't mean Coop and Maggie will hit it off. For all of your so-much-alikes, there's quite a few distinctions between you and Maggie. And as for Coop and me, things we have in common aren't necessarily things Maggie would find attractive."

"Well, I think they're perfect for each other."

He wasn't convinced, but he understood Liz's desire to make this happen. He remembered his first meeting with Lizzie. The broken Jimmy Choo shoe, mint jelly on toast—they seemed as different as two people could be. But it'd happened, and he never tried to analyze it. So, in truth, he had to admit, she might be onto something.

"I'm tired." He held back the bedding. "Come on."

She conceded her position, snuggling against him, her silk robe cool against his skin. Setting the covers lightly around them, he pulled her close. "Okay. If you're so sure, go ahead, but tread lightly."

CHAPTER SIX

Maybe Babysitting

Another Friday night, and instead of getting ready for a hot date, Maggie was going to review her third grader's stories about Christmas. Truth? She hadn't been on a date since Ricky. Between moving all the time and being scared out of her socks most of the time, the thought of meeting someone new and letting them get close to her? Ah, no.

Ricky was why she'd slammed the door on Nick Cooper. And how she wondered what he thought of her irrational behavior. *Stupid to even go there.* She did her best to put the handsome neighbor from her mind by organizing the kids' papers.

Teaching was a respectable profession, filled with lots of rewards, but she'd strayed far from her original career track. Her law school diploma was framed and hung next to the NYU bachelor's diploma. Like an afterthought, her teaching credential sat in a stand-alone frame at the end of her kitchen counter.

The two accomplishments that didn't hang on the wall were the framed license to practice law and the certificate allowing her to appear in federal court. Those were bubble-wrapped and tucked behind her rain boots in the back of the hall closet.

She thought about taking down the law degree, but it kept her humble, and it reminded her how easily life could spin out of control.

She stopped herself from going down that rabbit hole and shifted her focus to the mound of papers. This work should be enjoyable, and it was most of the time, but meeting Nick had muddled her brain. She kept imagining him knocking on her door, only this time, she wouldn't slam it in his face.

Looking down at the stories—resigned to a night alone, she pulled one out to review. The assignment would allow her to see where the kids stood in their skills development. There would be two follow-up submissions to review how the students had taken her direction. Also, the school had made the holiday stories into a contest. She was excited to possibly have the winning entry be a part of the Christmas pageant in December.

An hour into grading, Nick popped into her head again, and she was annoyed at her lack of mental discipline. He was no one to her, and, after her behavior, she felt certain he wouldn't be coming over for coffee and a chat anytime soon.

It'd been a warm day, so she'd opened the window on the east side of her apartment. New York City street noises filtered in with the sounds of life being lived. A life from which she'd been hiding for years.

She switched gears from grading papers to tidying up. Then, as if compelled, she went to the door with the crazy notion that she'd check the hallway to see if Nick was around. Nuts. Like he was wandering the hallway when he had a life and a kid. She opened the door, saw nothing, and, despite her concerns for Teddy Amato, decided to leave it open for a bit. She didn't kid herself—screw the heat excuse, maybe Nick *would* walk by. She stepped back while murmuring to herself, "I need a glass of wine."

"For what? To toast the serial killer who can't resist a little rape and murder when faced with an open door?"

Maggie took a step back. *Nick.* She hadn't thought opening the door for a moment would result in being pillaged. She'd barely glanced up and down the hall and intended to lock herself back into her sanctuary in mere minutes.

Her determination to deliver a rapier-like reply was thwarted by a constricted throat and a mouth too dry to speak.

He seemed unconcerned she was standing there, fish-mouthing. "I have it on good authority you're a smart, capable woman. But leaving your door open? Maybe not such a good idea."

She needed a brilliant response. Nothing bubbled forth. Then she realized his tone expressed concern. Perhaps she should kiss him instead.

"Never mind," he said. "I came to ask you a favor. I know, forward of me since we've barely met."

She studied his features and his somber expression. He stood straight, seemed calm and in control, but there was a melancholy that diffused any brightness she'd noted when he'd dealt with his precocious child. The image of him back then made it hard for her to remain distant now.

He took a couple of steps into her apartment and surveyed her space. "Small, but nice."

"I imagine your two plus two-point something with a patio and a view of the skyline has a much bigger feel to it."

He stepped farther into the room. "So you've been there."

"Well, quite a caravan of realtors and potential buyers came through for a couple of months. I was curious and took a look-see. To be honest, I got a little jealous, but I'm comfortable here. It fits my needs."

"I'm sure it does. It's cozy." Finishing his perusal, his gaze settled on Maggie. "Good natural light. You an artist?"

"No."

"I'm sorry."

"That I'm not an artist?"

"No. I guess we got off to a rough start. Sometimes I come on a little strong."

She mined for composure she didn't feel. "I slammed a door in your face."

"You did, didn't you?" He smiled.

She took metered breaths to keep from going weak in the knees and opened and closed her fists in an attempt to control her heart rate.

"You're not going to punch me, are you?" he asked.

"Oh." She relaxed her fists. "This?" She shook her arms. "It's an exercise I do all the time. It's like a yoga thing."

"I make you nervous."

"Not at all," she lied and put her hands behind her back. Another deep breath, in and out, as she tried to act as relaxed as he appeared to be.

"I was under the impression you were a teacher."

"Yet you asked if I was an artist—but teacher would be correct."

"Hmm." His smile widened, and dimples emerged on both cheeks. "Then you *are* good with kids."

"That's kind of jumping to conclusions. I mean, I could be a terrible teacher."

"I suppose." He turned his back and walked toward the wall with her diplomas. When he walked past her, she got a whiff of something woodsy. Maggie didn't usually like aftershave or cologne, but his was nice. A warm outdoorsy smell, like he should be in a flannel shirt and blue jeans instead of a tailored suit.

Well, he'd taken off the jacket, maybe when he first got home, and his tie was loose in a careless, unintentionally sexy way. He wore a tucked-in fitted shirt and a smart leather belt highlighting his flat stomach and... She kept her gaze from traveling down any farther than the belt.

"Law degree? What for?" he asked.

Funny. She'd been thinking the same thing moments earlier. She was bothered he'd interrupted her fantasy while studying his perfect backside. "Why not?"

"Well, it seems like a lot of serious study for someone who ends up—"

"A school teacher?" She took a breath. "I stick to a goal. One of those was law school. But then it dawned on me: I didn't want to work a hundred hours a week for five years in some firm where the required dress code cost more than a newbie's salary. Turns out, I didn't really like the law." She inhaled, held the breath in, clenched and unclenched her fists again, exhaled, and then waited for him to realize she was lying through her teeth.

"You're cute when you get defensive."

Even if she had a perfect retort, which she didn't, she opted for misdirection. "I jog."

His gaze roamed from her face before traveling down to her toes as if to confirm his impression from her wardrobe—she'd bet he was thinking schoolmarm-ish and not in that sexy, flattering fantasy way—and, yes, she was a runner.

Maggie felt a drop of perspiration above her lip but refused to swipe it away. She tried walking past him to get back to her work table, but he stopped her with a light grip on her arm.

"I'm sorry. I'm interrupting you." He released her arm and motioned to the piles of paper. "You must have things to do. Since losing my wife…"

It seemed he was still practicing saying those words. She understood and recognized sorrow and instinctively knew he'd crumble with the slightest push.

"Sometimes," he continued, "I feel awkward around people. I'm not good yet"—he paused—"at being a single father. And that's not an excuse, I'm—"

Don't do it, Mags. Don't fall for the single dad bit.

But she did. And for a moment, she thought her body would disobey her brain, and she'd pull him into her arms.

This close, and in good light, she saw he wasn't as old as she'd first thought.

"I should go."

He didn't leave.

***

Nick wasn't sure why he hadn't noticed how tall she was the other day. Maybe it'd been the bear slippers. Koalas? Yeah, that was it. Or because he'd had Em to deal with, the little tyrant, leaving the apartment without his permission or his knowledge. Then again, maybe it was having a door slammed in his face that clouded his memory.

Standing near Maggie now, he saw she was at least five foot ten, maybe five-eleven.

"I'd like to start over, Ms. Reynolds, if it's possible?"

"Why? I mean, did you do something wrong?"

Nick took a small step back to make her more comfortable. "Whatever I did to warrant you slamming the door in my face? That's why we're starting over."

"Oh. That." She was clenching her fists again, and he blamed his proximity.

"Yes, that." She laughed, and when she did, her eyes sparkled. "I remembered I had a phone appointment scheduled with the school's principal."

He stepped closer again. "He or she must be highly intolerant if your timing had to be so precise." Nick recognized her answer as a lie. Maybe not an outright lie, but at least an attempt to steer him away from the subject or to let him off the hook.

"Well, she is a stickler. We call her Simon Legree."

"No, you don't."

"You're right. We don't. But slamming the door in your face? It's not worth the details. It is, however"—she took a deep breath—"worthy of an apology. I'm sorry for being rude."

"Apology accepted." Nick was still certain she was dodging the truth. Something else was going on in her life, and whatever it was, it made her jumpy. She seemed leery of anything and anyone invading her space. He thought briefly of the strange envelope he'd handed her the other day. Of course, being in her apartment made her uncomfortable, but for some insane reason, he couldn't back away.

"Which brings me to why I showed the other day," he said, "and why I'm here now. I was hoping you could, on occasion, help me with Emily. It was Liz Willis's suggestion."

Inexplicably drawn to Maggie, he inched even closer.

This woman was nothing like his quiet, petite, blonde Meg. Nothing. He found it impossible to believe there could be any kind of connection between him and Maggie, except perhaps a wave in the hallway, an agreement to pick up mail for a week, a borrowed cup of milk, or the reason he was in her apartment now: babysitting.

"To be honest?" he continued. "I can't think of one reason why you'd help me out, but Liz seemed to think you might, so—"

She dropped her head, which allowed Nick a moment to re-assess her attire. The short-sleeved cotton shirt was fitted and accentuated her shape. Lean, but with all the right curves. The skirt was a little frumpy, but she had great legs and slim ankles. The pumps were modest, which made sense, given her height. He realized her hair, held back in a kind of pony tail thing, half dangling, half attached somehow to her head, wasn't quite brunette or blonde. A hint of red highlights gleamed from waning sunlight coming in through the window.

His fingers twitched, and he had to hold back the urge to reach out and free her hair to tumble around her shoulders. Her smile dazzled him, and that wasn't a thought he'd had about anybody in two years. Feelings he hadn't dreamed could ever exist again surfaced and blasted through every nerve ending in his body.

He wanted to pull her against him, hold her, but he didn't dare. She'd no doubt freak out, and he'd be beyond control. Another thing he hadn't experienced in years.

"Liz suggested I meet you, perhaps get to know you a bit over lunch, mostly because we're neighbors. I mean, yes, the babysitting thing came up, but it wasn't the main focus." He stepped closer again. "I mean, it seemed reasonable enough."

"It is," she whispered.

"Come again?"

She raised her head and stared, making him feel like a bug under a microscope. "It is a reasonable request."

Neither of them moved.

Then he took a step back. He wondered why the ache in his groin, a sensation he hadn't experienced in a long time, lingered. *Move, Coop.* He was afraid if he didn't, he wouldn't be able to. Studying her, he realized she'd been as dumbfounded as he was at their reaction to each other. He was sure of it.

"My number, both home and office, are on this card." He reached into his wallet and pulled out the card, then placed it on the cluttered table. Knowing he should go, he stayed.

He glanced at a child's drawing of a big green elf, at least he thought it was an elf, and saw encouraging notes in the margins of a hand-written page.

Stepping back, he asked, "So it's okay, then? I can call you about babysitting?"

She turned and stood straight, pushing her shoulders back. "Sure. I won't be surprised when you tell me you already have my phone number."

Nick grinned. "No, you shouldn't be. Liz thinks of everything."

"You're not wrong."

He'd made it to the front door. "If you need anything..." He paused at her door, thinking to say something else, but there was too much to say, and nothing to say.

He pulled the door shut and crossed the hall to his apartment.

CHAPTER SEVEN

Maggie's Demons

"I will," she answered him, but she was speaking to a closed door. She felt like punching a wall.

She also felt weak in the knees.

"Damn it." She'd let him get to her, which violated a rule she'd held staunchly in place for the last four years. The Post-Ricky rules. There were two: Never-Date-Gorgeous-Men and Don't-Hook-Up-With-Wannabe-Rock-Stars.

Nick fit the first category.

He'd made her feel wobbly. Unsure of herself. And yet, oddly comfortable. "What the hell?" She relived the moment when she was sure he was going to kiss her.

In that light-speed moment when the air between them sizzled with heat, she'd wanted him to. She needed to talk to Liz and give her a what-for. No. She needed to thank her for this opportunity to maybe move forward. After all, during the first years after her divorce, Maggie had chewed Liz's ear, ruminating over the past. But more recently, she'd been upbeat, not discussing her horrible marriage. Like she was getting back to normal.

Until Teddy started calling her, she'd actually been proud of herself. She'd worked hard to put that dark, disastrous time behind her. Now, with the Teddy specter hanging over her head, she was dizzy from going back and forth between reality and what was and obvious Liz's set-up attempt.

Liz lived her novels a little too much. Which was fine for *her* life, but she should know better than to try to drop that nonsense on Maggie's head. She should be at least a bit angry with Liz for giving out her telephone number to a complete stranger. Except now it didn't matter because Maggie felt like getting to know her neighbor was a good idea. Nick had managed to stir up sensations long locked away; even some she swore she'd never felt in her life.

Her brain was melting down with the back-and-forth conversation in her mind, so, shaking her head, she went to the kitchen sink. After splashing water on her face, she patted her skin dry with a dish towel. Mistake. The thing stunk. She realized she was behind on everything, including laundry. She pulled back the folding doors to her apartment-size stackable washer and dryer. Thinking to gather up a load, she did a nose check of her underarms.

"Oh. My. God. I stink."

Could he smell me?

She walked, muttering, into the bathroom, where she grabbed the PJs hung on the hook and caught a glance of herself in the mirror. "Well, happy shit." She studied herself a few moments longer, trying to find something redeeming in the reflection.

Instead, she saw a tired school teacher, eye makeup worn off, hair askew. "Damn it. Is that a coffee stain?" *Yep.* Her Ann Taylor blouse needed a visit to the dry cleaner.

"Okay, then." She turned and left the bathroom.

If the handsome GQ man widower dad had gotten a whiff of her, let alone seen the end-of-day mess she lived in, she could probably forget having lunch with him, even if it was to discuss babysitting.

"Liz. How could you do this to me?" The ceiling fan didn't answer.

Besides, Maggie knew.

One, there was her best friend's penchant for matchmaking. Two, she knew Liz wanted only the best for her. In retrospect, it was odd that for all the years they'd known each other, Liz had never set up Maggie with anyone. Nope. Maggie had found Ricky all on her own, and given that disaster, the idea of her dating again wasn't "who" but "if ever."

She shoved the stuff she'd gathered into the stackable washer and closed the lid, making a mental note to add what she was wearing—except the blouse—and run the machine later in the evening.

"Papers, not stewing. Papers, not laundry." She marched to the table where she'd been working, repeating the mantra.

Resituated, she reached for pen and pencil. On a scrap of paper, she wrote: "1) Get through five stories 2) Shower 3) Start load of laundry, and 4) WINE."

Damn, but I'm organized.

She wasn't, but she was entitled to a little self-affirmation after the Nick encounter.

***

Maggie was drawing a thumbs-up on the last page of Mark Brown's story, adding, "What a terrific illustration of Santa's rocket, Mark. A clever re-do of *The Night Before Christmas,* little green men and all. I'm looking forward to your next draft."

Odd how she could get so engrossed after putting off the task for so long. She surveyed the pile of paperwork. Comparing the "to-do" stack with her "done" pile, she saw she was halfway through. "I'm winning." With a fist pump, she snapped up one of the few remaining cubes of Gouda cheese and popped it into her mouth. The aqua-colored serving plate was evidence she'd eaten dinner: three cheese bites, two whole wheat crackers, a quarter of an apple, and a well-licked spoon that no longer held any peanut butter.

Her wine glass was empty, but the bottle was still half full and in the fridge. A testament to how involved she'd become in her students' papers.

She raised her arms straight up, palms toward the ceiling, and stretched to release the kink in her spine. With a turn of her head, she braced against her own rank smell, remembering she'd sat with the wine and dinner, intending to shower after five papers.

"Yuck, Maggie. Guess it's into the shower, another glass of wine, and"—she shoved back from the table—"a little TV before falling asleep."

The entire time she'd been working on the Christmas stories, it seemed the world had gone quiet, which was silly. It was New York City, and her window was still open. She must've been more engrossed than she'd thought as now the sounds she'd grown to love filtered up from the busy street. A far-off siren, horns honking, a hum of activity, things that couldn't be specifically identified—noises that were there pretty much all the time.

She loved it and supposed the sounds of NYC had the same impact on her as playing a white noise tape might have on someone else. Bonus? She didn't have to pay for an app on her phone for the experience.

Leaving the desk light on to prevent slamming into something when she came back for her bedtime slug of chardonnay, she took her dinner plate to the kitchen, scraped the remnants of her dinner into the garbage disposal, and tucked the plate into the dishwasher.

She double-checked the locks, all three of them, and was turning to head to her bedroom when she heard muffled noises outside her door.

Quietly, she squinted through the peephole and got a glimpse of Emily circling her father in the hallway. The girl was chattering about the characters in a play.

He took his daughter to the theatre?

She couldn't stop herself from staring when Nick turned, and she swore he looked straight at her and winked.

No way. She was imagining things.

But when he opened his door, she heard, "Emily, go straight in and start getting ready for bed. I'm right behind you."

Maggie didn't catch Emily's reply, but what she did hear rocked her.

"Goodnight, Ms. Reynolds. Sweet dreams."

**

The scream woke Maggie. She bolted upright, her hands digging into the couch pillow. Then she swatted at something, semiconscious, the vision so real.

In a daze, she didn't know who'd screamed. It seemed close, as if in the room.

She took deep breaths, and as her entire brain came back online, she realized she'd been the one who screamed.

"It can't be you, Ricky. It can't be."

Tears were streaming down her face. She was shaking and must've been sweating because her t-shirt was soaked. She picked up her cell phone and saw it was two a.m. Shit. She'd fallen asleep on the sofa.

At this hour, Ricky would've been walking through the door, banging into furniture because he was drunk. That had been his M.O. more often than not during the last two years of their relationship, and on and off the rest of the years they'd been together. That was when the abuse would start, and yet she always forgave him. The dark wavy hair, the blurry blue eyes, and that smile. The goofy grin that sucked her in every time, even when she was furious. Even after a sweet "Hey, babe" right before he turned into a complete shit.

No, that wasn't correct. A monster.

Being raped by her own husband. More than once. She shuddered. The only person she'd ever shared any of that with was Liz.

Maggie looked around in the dim light to confirm she was in her own apartment, everything was all right, and it'd been a nightmare of the dream variety. Nothing more.

The half-empty glass of chardonnay sat where she'd left it on the coffee table. She grabbed it and slugged down the warm contents.

She'd been a dammed lawyer, a good one. Accomplished and capable, yet she'd been unable to get out from under the brutally abusive relationship Ricky Amato established once his ring was on her finger.

To this day, she still couldn't figure out how she allowed it to happen. She knew it happened to other women. She wasn't alone. But in happening to her? Maggie labeled it a weakness, a flaw in her character.

But he was long gone from her life, and now in a permanent way: dead and buried. At least the nightmares had lessened over the years. Until now. She tried to remember when she had the last vivid one, and it had been months. She rubbed her eyes and talked to the ceiling fan again. "Ricky's dead, Mags."

So, why the nightmares now?

Teddy.

Uncertain she'd ever lose the terror of her past when she was visited by such horrific nightmares, she stood and took the glass to the kitchen.

There were no pictures of Ricky anywhere.

Well, not entirely true. He'd been a part of her life, and that meant family gatherings and office get-togethers. She knew in the photo albums beneath extra blankets stored in the hope chest at the end of her bed—and that was a stupid name for it, a *hope* chest—that a turn of any page may include him. Smiling up from the sofa, or with a Christmas tree in the background, him leaning against a doorjamb, a beer in one hand and wearing a sardonic grin.

So many pictures with the famous Ricky Amato.

And that grin.

The grin that preceded a hard twist of her arm. Or before dragging her out of a dinner chair onto the floor.

Or maybe that special smile that segued into a kick in her gut once she was down.

She shivered at the memories and moments like these when the images were so real she could hear Ricky's breathing behind her, around her, over her.

She could no longer deny the mystery caller was Teddy, and she needed to tell someone, but who? She didn't want to burden Liz and Jake. And surely not her baby brother, Eric. He'd ride in, guns blazing. She had to keep Eric out of all things Ricky, or Eric would wind up in jail, and she couldn't allow that to happen.

Even though she'd never do it, she bet if she told Nick, he'd let her unburden herself, and then he'd assist her in getting help to keep Teddy out of her life.

Was that a knock at the door?

She looked at her phone again. 2:04. She must be hearing things.

Nick's gentle expression swam before her eyes like a hologram running in her head. He'd been so sweet with his child, and he had a good job and, apparently, a good marriage. It must've been. During the few brief interactions between them, she'd recognized the sorrow running beneath his "I'm okay" expressions.

And, had it really only been a few minutes since she woke up screaming? "I need a cat. An attack cat." She wondered if she could train a kitten to scratch someone's eyes out.

The sound of a thump, like something hitting the door, startled Maggie.

"Oh, God. There *is* someone outside my door," she mumbled in a whisper so low, she barely knew she'd voiced a thought.

Her imagination was running wild. Yeah. It definitely had to be her imagination.

She shook it off. She'd double-bolted and locked the door. Day doorman Max's counterpart would be on duty downstairs.

"Damn it, I left the window open."

Calm down, Mags. You're on the fifth floor. There's no fire escape outside your window.

When she'd cleaned out Ricky's stuff, she'd kept his baseball bat. Where was the damn bat? Shit. It was in the hall closet, next to the front door.

Steadying herself, she stood and slammed a knee on the coffee table. "Ouch." *Idiot.* She reached down to rub her knee but jerked up when she heard a different kind of noise.

Someone yelling.

Someone yelling her name.

On the other side of her door.

CHAPTER EIGHT

Late-Night Visitor

"Ms. Reynolds." The thump she'd heard was, in fact, knocking. Well, pounding. The threat on the other side was not a bad person trying to kill her. Nope. That voice belonged to her handsome neighbor.

"Ms. Reynolds, are you in there? Are you all right?" He pounded on her door again. "Answer me, or I'm kicking this door down."

"Hold on," she shouted to the closed door, secretly wanting him to try to do as promised. Though she didn't think he'd manage. Not with all her NYPD-approved locks. "I'm okay. Hang on a second."

She skirted the end of the sofa, and because she was in a hurry, she slammed her right shin into the corner of the coffee table. "Mother f—" She bit her tongue and went down like a rock. On the way down, she scraped the outside of her right thigh on the same from-hell corner. "Ow, damn it." She started by rubbing her shin, but feeling something running down her leg, she reached up to feel the skin where she'd struck her thigh. "I'm bleeding."

"What? Are you all right in there, Reynolds?"

"Hold on." She'd left half an oatmeal cookie on a napkin smack in the middle of her table. She tugged at it, put the cookie in her teeth, and pressed the paper against her thigh. "Com…" With the cookie between her teeth, she couldn't talk, so she swallowed it. "…ing."

She scooched across the floor, reached up, and unlocked the first deadbolt, then paused. Her brain was dealing with the pain from the recent injuries and a whopper of a nightmare. Better to err on the side of caution. "Who is it?"

"It's Nick. Nick Cooper, your neighbor."

"How can I be sure?" She couldn't help it since he had slipped into a banging-on-the-door-at-two-in-the-morning crazy person.

"I can wake up Em and have her vouch for me."

She laughed at an image of Emily in wild PJs, hair no doubt sticking out every which way and rubbing sleep from her eyes.

Maggie reached up and tugged open the second deadbolt. A flash of what she might look like delayed her releasing the final turn. A swipe across her face resulted in cookie crumbs on her shirt, so she gave up.

"Maggie, open the damned door."

For some reason, his switch from bossy to demanding had her picturing him shirtless and in a tight pair of faded jeans.

"Damn it, Reynolds. Now."

Okay. He sounded pissed. But not in a threatening way. In a "Woman, you're a pain in my ass" way.

The last thing she thought of when turning the bottom lock was she was in her worst pair of worn-out running shorts and a tie-dyed tank shirt that was a little too snug.

***

Nick fell into and over her when she finally yanked open the door. "What the hell?" He disengaged from their unintended clench, stood, and hovered over her. "You are the most exasperating woman I've ever met." He looked around and then down. "What the hell are you doing on the floor?"

"You demanded I open the door." Her eyes were wider than he remembered, and her pupils were dilated due to the dim light.

"I did, and with good reason."

She didn't budge. Nick wondered if he should go all chivalrous and help her up, but, for the moment, he opted to maintain his distance. Things still seemed dodgy.

Without getting up, she reached to close the door, but he grabbed it and stopped her. "Emily's asleep, and though I locked my door, I don't want her waking up and deciding she needs to start a search party."

"How does a seven-year-old muster up a search party?"

In spite of the awkward circumstances, he laughed. It seemed Maggie had a sense of humor. "Let's see. *My* seven-year-old dons her cowgirl holster and boots and musters up, I would expect, as many stuffed animals as she can carry to the front door."

"She's a smart kid."

"She is indeed."

"Takes after you, I suppose."

"I will concede some similarities, but she has more people smarts than I have, or will likely ever have." He hated that he was staring down at Maggie, thinking about ways to help her up without it seeming aggressive.

"Ah."

"Ah, what?"

"An admission against interest, that." She smiled, then turned her attention to her right thigh, which he couldn't help but notice was sinewy and shapely.

"That sounds like your law school talking."

"Sort of. I lied earlier today."

"About what? Is the diploma a fake?"

"No. Not a fake."

"So you say."

"I *was* a lawyer."

"What?"

She turned to one side and pushed off the floor, but not before she yelped from the sharp pain in her kneecap. "As in a practicing lawyer. You know, big office, files, court appearances, that kind of lawyer."

"I'd love the details on that, but right now, you need help."

"Golly gee, I can't keep anything from you, can I?"

"Well, you had me snowed about your reasons not to pursue the practice of law after spending three years in school trying to do that very thing. And quit changing the subject. Where are you hurt?"

Hopping on one foot, she got to the kitchen and leaned against the counter. After flicking a switch beneath the countertop, the kitchen flooded with light. Nick had to take a deep breath and bite his tongue. His neighbor was hot. There was no other way to put it.

All five feet—and now he was sure—eleven inches of her, lean muscles wrapped in flawless skin. Unless one counted freckles as a deduction, and he didn't. He'd been correct in his earlier observation: there were auburn highlights in her mat of hair, this time jammed upon her head with a big clip. He still wanted to see all that hair down.

The running shorts were faded and worn nearly thread-bare, and her t-shirt was an invitation: tie-dyed, maybe washed one too many times, it clung to her form, leaving no doubt as to the shape of her breasts and the flat hallow of her stomach.

"I bruised my left knee earlier," she said. "Then I tripped over the coffee table, which attacked my shin, after which I lost my balance, fell, and took a chunk out of my thigh. You get the picture, right?"

He did, and in a way, Nick wished he hadn't missed it. Looking back at the coffee table, he said, "It's glass. You should cut out tennis balls for the corners."

"Okay," was all she said.

"Okay, what?"

"Your fatherhood is showing."

He smiled, but then his gaze landed on her thigh. "Oh, hell, Reynolds. You're bleeding."

She laughed, and it filled the empty space between them, a space he felt compelled to close, although he didn't think the timing was quite right.

He reminded himself attraction to women led to heartbreak, agony, anger, a spectrum of emotions he'd sworn off from the day of Meg's diagnosis, through the seven months of her treatment, the failure of all medical efforts to save her, and then, the inevitable.

His beautiful Meg dying. Her pain. Her loving him right up to the last moment. To the final breath while holding his hands when she'd smiled with an acceptance he'd never found.

Not then, and not in the two years that followed.

"Hey, you still with me?"

"Yeah, sorry. Thinking."

"It's only a little blood."

"So I see. Do you have a first aid kit?"

"Top shelf of the closet by the front door."

Nick turned, and a good thing too, because watching her and her goofy grin while wearing invitational nighttime clothing caused more than the twinge that'd happened yesterday. This time, he had a full-blown reaction below the waist for the first time since Meg got sick.

While Maggie was studying her wound, he was trying to think of anything but her, stalling as he stared into her closet for the first aid stuff, waiting for his body to return to a "nothing doing" status.

Everything about her seemed disorganized, and he expected the closet to be as chaotic as she was.

But, to his surprise, the closet was OCD compared to what he'd witnessed in their earlier brief but memorable encounters. Coats, by size and purpose, then sweaters, in descending color from light to dark, on fat hangers. Rainboots and tennis shoes, side by side on the floor, a folded blanket and extra pillow stacked on a shelf to one side. As directed, a first aid kit sat in its designated spot to the left of the pillow.

As he reached for the kit, it struck him that he too wore sleep clothes. He was glad he'd thought to put on a t-shirt over his plaid pajama bottoms before rushing across the hall. As he turned to play doctor to her wound, he realized he still had no clue what'd caused her to scream so loud and with such anguish he'd heard her from his balcony.

***

Maggie hiked herself onto the bar and allowed Nick to study her wound, his fingers gently pushing at the skin to determine what? She didn't know. Maybe to ascertain whether stitches were needed.

She studied the top of his head, taking in his thick hair, which begged tousling. She ordered her hands not to reach out and instead focused on the occasional strand of grey here and there that made him sexy as hell.

Well, that and the way his PJ bottoms hugged his hips and the tight t-shirt revealed a workout body when he'd reached up to the top shelf of the closet.

"I don't think you need stitches." He continued to dab at the wound with one of those packaged towelette things. He'd already cleaned off the dribble of blood that went from mid-thigh to her kneecap. "See?"

She watched the path of his finger as it pressed gently against either side of the gash.

"But I can get you to the ER if you want to go," he added.

"Hell no. Patch me up. I'll be fine."

Maggie could see the wound was clean and dry but still seemed to want to bleed a little. He dabbed it again, and she had to focus over his shoulder because he was holding her calf with one hand while he worked, and she had that fuzzy brain sensation she almost forgot she'd enjoyed when a man had his hands on her.

"Hmm."

"Hmm, what? Is there something wrong?"

"What?" He looked up. The cool blue of his gaze slammed into her, and she couldn't look away. His hand held her leg steady, which was good. Essential. If he let go, she'd slide off the counter and land on her ass at his feet.

"Well, you said, 'hmm,' and I said, 'hmm, what?' and now you've said, 'what,' but you see, the way you said, 'hmm,' it sounded like there was something wrong. I mean, wrong with my leg."

"Nope, nothing wrong with your leg." He smiled. "But do you always make things so complicated?"

Wham. Proverbial freight train. Between his eyes, his smile, his broad shoulders, and his warm hand still holding her calf, she worried something inappropriate would happen.

The things she was thinking about doing came under the cataclysmic mistake category. Like slipping from the counter and into his arms.

From there to the couch, and from there to—"Stop."

"Now? Reynolds, don't be a baby. I'm almost done."

She'd said "stop" out loud. She was sure she'd thought it in her head.

She felt the loss of his warmth the moment he let go of her leg. He was fastidiously opening a medium-sized Band-Aid. She thought the gash warranted some cotton gauze and tape. *And a reward for being such a good girl.*

She shivered. By accident. Her body reacted to his final touch as he secured the bandage. Her response to him defined stupid.

"Oh, wow, you're cold. I'm sorry." He looked around. "Here." He'd grabbed a blue throw from the back of the sofa—the same one she'd had a mini-fantasy about—and covered her shoulders. "There."

Just like that, her hero turned all matter-of-fact, sweeping up the little debris left from his triage effort.

He was so near she swore she could smell good soap. Maybe he showered at night? The idea of him in the shower made her heart race.

She must've swooned or something because he reached out and held her hand. "Hang on. Let's get you off the counter and to your divan."

"My what?" Talking was difficult since she couldn't breathe.

"Oh, ah, sorry, the couch." Maggie slid from the counter, and he shadowed her to the sofa. "Emily and I have been playing a word game this whole week. We pick any object in the room and point to it. The other person has to come up with as many different words for it as possible, in, like, say, ten seconds." He sat her down with a gentle push on her shoulders. "It's silly, but that's the kind of thing dads do, I guess."

"You guess?"

"Well, when my wife, Meg, stopped working to spend those first few years with Emily, I was the come-home-tired dad. You know how it is."

She didn't. But it meant that instead of pillaging Maggie after her not-so-near-death experience, he had returned to Gorgeous-But-A-Dad guy from across the hall.

It struck her then: why had he been pounding on her door in the middle of the night?

She glanced up and thought she caught a look of concern. Was he conflicted? *Come on, Mags. He's got a kid across the hall.* Kids would come first, of course, and she didn't begrudge Emily having a responsible dad. A single dad.

"You should go," she said. "Emily shouldn't be alone."

Letting him off the hook was the right thing to do. Except he smiled, running a hand through his hair, the white t-shirt stretching up to reveal a flat belly. A quick glance at the tie-string to his plaid pajama pants, and all she could think was that slip of a cord was the only obstacle between her and... She heard a DJ record screech in her head.

"I'll check on you tomorrow, Reynolds. There's some details I want to go over with you about your past. That is *if* you'd consider babysitting Emily?"

"What do you mean, questions about my past?"

"C'mon, would I be a responsible dad if I didn't check out your character?"

"You have Lizzie's recommendation."

"That's true."

He'd ducked his head so she couldn't see his face, and it was driving her nuts. Was he kidding? Of course she'd babysit Emily. It meant being closer to him or getting closer. Maybe. As if she really wanted to. Not. Too many complications. Too likely he or his brilliant daughter would learn something about her she didn't want anyone to know. Like Ricky. And Teddy.

He was still standing over the couch, but now he looked at her straight on. She could see he was struggling to keep from laughing.

"You were kidding about the credentials thing," she said.

"A little bit, yeah. I already have glowing reports from Liz and my boss. So, will you? Sit for me?"

"I'd be happy to. But it has to coincide with my schedule."

"Oh, no problem. It wouldn't be often."

She hoped that when he did ask her, it would be for something other than dates with other women. Maggie wasn't sure why, but the idea of him with another woman made her a little crazy. It couldn't be jealousy. How could she be jealous of some woman she hadn't met being with a man she barely knew?

The light was low, but she thought his face reddened. Embarrassment? Discomfort?

Nick turned to the door and stopped. "My phone."

"I didn't know you brought it with you." For sure she couldn't see any place to hide the damn thing.

"Never leave Em without it."

"Oh, right. Sorry. Guess that's a ding in my babysitting credentials."

"Seriously? No, it was in my hand when we...uh, I tumbled through the door."

A flush of heat rushed through her. "Let me help you look." She tried to get off the sofa.

"No. Stay put."

He bent under the coffee table, and she found herself with a perfect view of his superior behind. He turned on his knees, and if she'd wanted to, she could reach out and almost touch him.

His phone was under the coffee table. He held it up like at trophy. "Found it."

Maybe thirty minutes had passed since she'd flung open the door and he'd landed in her living room.

"I'm curious," she asked because she wanted to know, and she wanted to stop him from leaving. "Why did you come over and pound on my door?"

"I thought I heard you scream."

"How? I mean, if I did scream, how would *you* hear it through doors, and halls, and walls, and stuff?"

Nick motioned with his head to the open window. "I couldn't sleep and was sitting on the balcony staring at the sky. I guess you had a bad dream? Anyway, I heard it, couldn't ignore it, and then...well, here we are."

"I'm sorry."

"Don't be. Was it a bad dream?"

"Yeah. One of those falling ones, you know?"

He didn't look like he believed her, but he let it go. "I'm glad you'll try babysitting Em. She seems to think you're the best thing since—"

"Sliced bread?"

"You're too kind. Sacrificing yourself to save me from saying something so trite."

"It's the least I could do."

Out came the boyish grin and his relaxed demeanor returned. Maggie was in serious trouble.

His accidental brush against her skin, his purposeful application of first aid, the fact that he'd gone all knight-in-shining-armor on her, and his giving her a taste of his warmth: she was smitten.

He was standing with the door open, silhouetted by the light in the building's hallway. She noticed the quick glance at his apartment door—worry for his daughter since it wasn't likely he was torn about leaving Maggie. Oh, but she wished.

"Listen, Reynolds."

Maggie didn't protest. In fact, she liked him using her last name. Like they shared a comradery of sorts. "I'm listening."

"I'm not sure what gave you the nightmare, but I hope you'll feel comfortable enough to share it with me in the light of day." He didn't give her time to say anything because as the door was closing, he said sharply, "Lock this door, all three ways."

After hopping across the room, she followed his instructions. He must've counted the number of locks when she was struggling to let him in, which seemed a lifetime ago.

Feeling like a teenage girl, she lay on the sofa and pulled the throw over her. With her hand resting on her wound, the place he'd touched her, she drifted off.

***

Quickly, Nick checked on Emily. His daughter slept soundly, and her cell phone rested on top of the covers. Her favorite doll was clasped between her two small hands. She was asleep and none the wiser for his disappearance. Still, he'd left her alone, albeit to help a neighbor, and it filled him with an elevated sense of worry and guilt, especially since Meg was gone.

I'm sorry, Meg. Sorry he couldn't save her. Sorry he didn't notice the changes—the circles under her eyes, the weight loss, how she'd push food away, and the worst? The grimaces she thought he didn't see when they made love. So many signs, silent cries against the pain she must've been feeling and would never mention. Sorry for everything.

He poured himself a single shot of whiskey and headed for a cold shower—the latter in disbelief because even when the frigid water slapped his body out of its stupor, he still ached with need.

Which made him nervous and excited. Beneath these new, or more accurately, forgotten sensations, was the constant echo of loss fading.

Everyone, including Emily, was anxious for Nick to move on. "Setting me up? Really?" he questioned the mirror, studying his face, but not seeing any changes.

Maybe Jake and Liz were right. He could trust their insight. Liz knew Meg as well as anyone could. So, when Liz said for the twentieth time, "Meg wouldn't want you to disappear from life; she'd want you to embrace it, if for no other reason than to show Emily there are so many reasons to be happy," he had to take a good look in the mirror and ask himself what he was waiting for.

But Maggie? Goofy, secretive Maggie was the one who reignited his spark? True, she was beautiful, though not in the poetry way. She was definitely not sonnet material, but she stirred something in his soul.

Quirky. Someone so *not* Meg, he couldn't think of anyone in his acquaintance who was more different.

How many times had he stood wrapped with a towel around his waist with Meg sitting on the toilet seat, talking about real-life things in the midst of their morning routines? Or Meg stepping out of the shower, tempting him, or telling him to hurry because she needed the sink?

But these images of Meg had started to fade, and most recently were replaced by a few encounters between him and his new neighbor.

He shook his head.

Meg was gone. Really gone.

Nick stared into the mirror, seeing flesh and bone and realizing that although Meg was dead, he was not.

CHAPTER NINE

Babysitting

Six a.m. and Maggie's cell phone was ringing. Nobody would call this early on a Saturday morning except terrifying Teddy.

Her resolve to talk to someone about the calls was gelling. Teddy had stepped up his campaign to disrupt her life. His threats were the same, but as the number of calls increased, they felt more invasive than the already petrifying toxicity.

Her heart was racing when she picked up the phone.

"Reynolds?"

Hearing Nick's voice, her heart kept racing.

It'd been a week since he'd done his two-in-the-morning Sir Lancelot schtick. Since then, they'd had a few quick chats in the hallway. And on Thursday, he'd been nonchalant when he suggested Saturday might work for their get-to-know-each-other lunch.

Now here he was on the phone at a near-abusive hour for a Saturday morning.

"Well, who else would it be?" she answered, a little peeved he'd think someone else might answer her phone. Of course, she'd have been equally insulted if he'd assumed she spent every night alone.

Which she did.

"Emily's sick."

Maggie bolted upright. "I'm so sorry. What can I do? Are you going to the hospital? Does she have a fever? How high? Or is it stomach flu? Is she vomiting—"

"Whoa, Maggie. Settle down."

"That's a term you use with a horse."

"Funny, Reynolds. It's not what you think. She woke up with a cold."

"Oh. That's not bad, then, is it?"

"Not unless her father has an important meeting this morning."

Maggie wondered if the day would come when she'd get to call him Coop, as she'd heard Liz do on occasion. "Uh-huh."

"And my regular gal—"

"Gal? Seriously?"

"Look, I need help. If you want to have a discussion with me about male chauvinism or whatever it is you think I'm guilty of, it'll have to be some other time."

"Right." Inappropriate time to be snarky. "I'm not sure why I'm being such a pill. Maybe it's the call out of left field at five-thirty in the morning?"

"Reynolds. I'm sorry." She heard a mix of chagrin and frustration in his voice. She wished she could see him and how he reacted to her.

She liked talking to him. Which could be more dangerous than neighborly. So, despite needing to start correcting her students' second drafts of their Christmas stories, and despite needing to clean her apartment—and despite the fact that her fridge was down to a couple of English muffins, a few slices of skinny Swiss cheese, a head of lettuce, the emergency canned coffee drinks, and the half jar of peanut butter with the wheat crackers on standby—she was ready to say "Yes" to his plea.

"When do you want me there?"

"You'll do it? Reynolds, you're a peach."

Peach? Really? How much older *was* Nick? That was something her dad would've said.

Still, she couldn't turn him down. Nick had come to her aid— hard to believe it was a week ago—and comforted her after a terrible nightmare *and* acted as her personal EMS tech. There weren't enough ways to thank him for what he'd done except perhaps to tell him the truth.

About Ricky. And Teddy. And the grand eff-up that was her life.

But how could she unload all of her crap on Nick? Gorgeous. Deep-voiced. Broad-shouldered. Successful. Tall. Tempting. Nick.

What was she leaving out? Oh, a good dad.

The recitation of his attributes matched the beat of her heart.

"So, it's okay, Reynolds. I get that it's short notice. Plus, I'm asking you to expose yourself to her cold, give up your Saturday." Silence. Maggie counted to ten and was about to say something when he chimed back in. "It's too much. I'll call—"

"Nick. It's okay. I'm exposed to billions of little kid germs on a daily basis. I can handle it."

"Should I bring her there?"

"Not unless you want to bring your fridge."

"Sorry?"

"I haven't been shopping this week. It's a bit nursery-rhyme-bare cupboards here. Besides, Emily should be in a familiar place. How much time do I have?"

"I have to head out at eight." He took a breath. "I'll be gone for probably four or five hours."

"No problem, and eight's fine. I can shower and wrangle a little breakfast before I need to come over."

"No need."

"To shower?" Maggie blushed and was grateful she and Nick weren't familiar enough to FaceTime.

She was surprised how much her composure failed at the sound of his voice. Not to mention—though now she was mentioning it to herself—thinking of the feeling of his touch on her skin.

The ease with which he'd inspected and cleaned the wound, and the few seconds it'd taken for him to secure the bandage to her thigh, would hardly qualify as more than medical ministration. But it didn't matter that the contact was brief and clinical. It'd rocked her, and it'd seemed alive with possibilities for a deeper connection.

"No. Of course you should shower." His voice had the kind of quality people looked for in movie stars or world leaders. She inhaled a deep breath that was supposed to give her courage and enough time to think up something brilliant to say. "I was referring to you getting some breakfast, Reynolds. Have you been to the coffee shop on the corner? I know the owner." *Of course you do.* "I ordered some pastries. They'll be delivered before I head out."

"Oh, okay. It's not exactly on my diet routine, but I could use a break."

"You're on a diet?"

"Yeah."

"Why? You're not overweight."

Another reason to like Nick. "Not now."

"Were you?"

She couldn't decide whether to credit him for being so open or smacking him for reminding her she'd struggled with her weight in high school. They were still strangers. He had no way of knowing her being pudgy until she sprouted into a bean pole her junior year was a sensitive subject.

She also figured there was no ill intent on his part, but all the buttons Ricky had pushed over the years buzzed around her brain like angry bees.

You're going to work like that? You look frumpy. I thought you were giving up cake?

God, she hated the reels in her head. Ricky was gone. Dead.

"You there, Reynolds?"

"Yep."

"As I was saying, I'm going to make sure there are pastries here for breakfast. You can go over the babysitting list with Emily. It helps to reinforce the rules with her."

"A babysitting list?"

"Sure. Rules. Dos and don'ts. Emily's a bit of a con artist. If she can figure a way, you'll eat cake and ice cream for lunch." Maggie thought she heard her new charge in the background, yelling something. "So, we'll see you at ten minutes to eight. That work?"

"Um, yeah. Sure. Fine. I'll need your number and where you'll be. Stuff like that." Maggie had a visual of sneaking up behind Nick, placing her hands over his eyes while he was trying to engage in some business conversation.

"Of course. I have the babysitting book on the counter for reference."

"Like a published book for babysitters?"

He laughed, and it came out like a rumble. She imagined if she was standing right next to him, the vibration would've travelled into her arms, down her legs, and gone to other, even better places.

"No. It's *my* book. Not *a* book. It's the list I mentioned. Things to do and watch out for with Emily."

Could she handle rules for sitting for a bright, sweet little kid like Emily? "Is there something you're not telling me? Is she allergic to something, or—I'm sorry to ask, but it's a need-to-know question—does she have behavioral problems?"

"God, no." Said in an explosion of laughter. "Of course not. I'm scaring you. It's me, I suppose. I function on schedules and rules, lists and more lists, and, well, it helps me handle things."

Maggie guessed that "things" had to do with losing his wife and being a single parent. Reassurance might be in order. "No worries. Who better than an elementary school teacher to know young children need structure."

He said nothing, and she again wished she could see his expression. Oh, hell, she could admit to herself she'd like to touch his face, rub the back of his neck, somehow ease the tension she knew came with him explaining how off balance he still was since his wife died.

"Nick?"

"Sorry. I was distracted. Emily's tugging on my arm—"

She heard the child's voice but couldn't make out what she was saying. Maggie could picture Emily with bedhead, saggy pajama bottoms, maybe a matching top. And having a cold, it would affect her appearance. In Emily's case, it would make her more ragamuffin-cute.

"Listen, Reynolds. I'll see you at ten to eight. Everything you need will be here. And, again, thanks. Your help will keep my schedule from getting jammed up next week."

He hung up.

The solitude of her apartment hit without warning. She imagined it would be like one of those earthquakes out in California. You're fine one moment, then the next, you're tossed onto the floor or maybe hanging onto a window frame from ten stories up.

The idea of quakes terrified her.

So did babysitting Emily.

And even more terrifying?

Falling for Emily's dad.

***

Maggie and Emily were sitting on the humongous, overstuffed sofa that ran against one wall of the living room and ended in a large chaise that made for the perfect child's nest. Emily was coloring with her feet straight out in front of her, repeats of SpongeBob episodes were playing on the big flat screen, and they'd already had lunch.

Maggie kept thinking Emily would nap after they'd eaten, but it turned out she was a bottomless pit when it came to food. After stuffing themselves with pastries at breakfast, at noon, on the dot, food was delivered, compliments of Nick.

At Emily's insistence, she and Maggie sat on the sofa and feasted on cheeseburgers with fries, including what Emily called a vegetable, but was actually an unfathomable amount of ketchup.

And Princess Em—as Emily had requested being called—hadn't slowed down a bit. The little girl was nowhere near taking a nap. So fell Rule One of babysitting.

Maggie, on the other hand, couldn't keep her eyes open and kept sipping at her diet cola as a cry for help.

Nick had insisted a nap was critical and further inferred all the other babysitters had no problem accomplishing the task. If he returned home at this moment, Maggie would have a black mark on the Cooper wall chart of babysitters' accomplishments.

"You know, Em—" The Princess arched her eyebrows and opened her mouth to correct Maggie. "I mean, Princess Em." Having received a royal handwave, Maggie proceeded. "This is my first babysitting job for you and your dad. I'd like it if both of you were pleased with my efforts. So, if you took a nap, I won't get a black mark for falling down on my duties."

Her young charge stopped coloring and resituated herself as if a very serious discussion was about to ensue. Emily placed each crayon back in her elaborate storage box for pens, pencils, erasers, etc., and after what felt like forever, the last art supply was back in place, and Emily had closed the coloring book.

"Thank you for putting all of that away, Princess."

"I can't color if I'm taking a nap."

"An astute observation."

"What's astute mean?"

"Um." Maggie hoped she could explain it without getting even more complicated. "It's the ability to assess people or situations correctly."

Emily pushed her back further against the pillows and folded her hands in her lap. "I see."

Maggie hoped that she didn't have to add to the definition and regretted the child's advanced command of the English language.

Emily grabbed the closest teddy bear and sat it on her lap. "It would be like if I knew a secret about something and I used it to get more popcorn?"

Maggie bit her lip to keep from bursting out laughing. Nick's daughter wasn't a con artist, but she was close. "Actually, Princess Em, that would be blackmail."

Emily's grin was wide, her cheeks puffed out like chipmunks, and her pixie ears were poking out from beneath pigtails. "Oh, that is bad."

What would it be like to live with a young Einstein? Nick and his wife must've known Emily was special. Maggie wondered about broaching the subject of Emily's mother, but that felt like a betrayal of Nick's trust.

"Do you like my dad?"

Emily's question startled Maggie. She'd been in her head while Emily obviously had been planning the question for the right time. "Well, sure. He's a nice man."

Emily squeezed the teddy bear. "But do you *like*, like him?"

Maggie believed in being honest with children, but this was on a level she didn't know how to handle. "What do you mean?"

"He likes you."

"He does?"

"Uh-huh." The articulation was gone, replaced by a seven-year-old child who'd lost her mother, moved into a new home, and, more likely than not, was subjected to the dark mood of an adult who was struggling with how to cope with his grief while keeping a brave face for his daughter.

"And if I did?" Maggie shifted positions so she was closer to Emily. "Would that be okay with you?"

"Oh, yes." Without a beat, Emily turned to Maggie and buried her face in Maggie's chest. Uncertain what to do, she rubbed Emily's back and listened as her breathing slowed.

She was asleep.

Maggie shifted the child's weight to the sofa, laying her flat, and placing one of the occasional pillows under her head, covered her with the blanket, tucking Emily's teddy bear under an arm.

Quietly, Maggie carried the remains of their meal to the trash, except for the unfinished milkshake, which fit on the door shelf of the fridge.

Looking around, since there were no more messes, she was going to run to use the restroom, but the distinctive noise of a key turning in the lock got her attention. Maggie didn't want Nick to wake his daughter, so she ran to the door to stop him from charging in with some sort of robust "Hello, I'm home. Where's my girls?"

Did I just think the "Where's my girls"?

She tugged on the door at the same time Nick pushed it open from the other side.

For someone else, it wouldn't've been inevitable that they would both stumble and end up prone on the floor, but for Maggie, it was. She took the brunt of the fall on one hip and looked up to see his face about three inches from hers as he lay above her.

"Cripes, Reynolds. What is it with you and doors?"

Maggie shushed him, pointing at the sofa while trying not to laugh. She couldn't help herself and covered her mouth with her hands, so the laugh came out more like a snort.

"It's not funny." It sounded fake stern, and he didn't move. She thought she could see him struggling to keep himself in check.

"Yeah, it is." She succumbed to another laughing fit, which ended in a hiccup.

His eyes were ridiculously blue, unlike the shadowy greyish-blue she'd noted in the hallway and her apartment. And this close up, she could see the parts of Emily that were from his DNA.

Strong nose, high cheekbones, the ability to raise one eyebrow. Emily could do it too, but on Nick, it was so damned captivating.

Maggie choked back another hiccup, waited, then took a breath and held it. It was only for a few seconds, but the hiccups stopped.

"She's asleep?" He angled his head in the direction of the living room sofa.

"As ordered."

"Ah, that wasn't really an order."

"No? It's written in three places, including an over-abundance of exclamation points in your notes and in all caps in the Babysitting Bible."

"Well, not every babysitter has been able to get her to take a nap."

"So you lied."

"I fudged. A little." This time, his smile was genuine. Emily had the same dimples as Nick. Maggie couldn't look away.

"Ah-ha." She felt the vibration of her non-verbal reply against his chest and wondered if he felt it too. His expression made it obvious that he had. His smile faded, her gaze locked with his, she didn't dare move. Though she couldn't even if she'd wanted to. Which she didn't.

It hit her at the same instant she saw it cross his face. Raw. Desire. All the air seemed to have left the room, but the flame between them didn't go out. His lips were so close if she tilted up, she could press hers against his. She held her breath, waiting.

"Hi, Daddy." Emily clamored off the couch and was standing over them in an instant.

Nick's smile was back, and his deep chuckle shook against Maggie's core. He raised himself with a push-up and got to his feet.

Maggie's disappointment was crushing, which was an overreaction to a fleeting possibility. Looking up, she saw his hand reaching out to help her. She didn't fight it.

She stood next to him while Emily stared up at them, a smile lighting up her face as her gaze swept back and forth between them.

Back and forth, the bear clutched in her little hands.

"Daddy?"

"Yes, baby."

"Do you think it's okay for Maggie to call you Coop now?"

"I do. Is it okay with you, Em?"

"Yup."

"Well, I guess it's unanimous, then."

Emily seemed to be rethinking her proposal. "No, it's not."

Nick looked at his daughter, then at Maggie. "Why not? It's you and me, and I agree with you. So why isn't that unanimous?"

Emily turned back and forth at her waist, the corners of her mouth barely turned up in a smile. "Maggie has to vote too."

"Oh, right." He beamed at his daughter, then turned to Maggie. "What do you say, Reynolds? You brave enough to call me Coop?"

I want to call you a hell of a lot more than that.

Maggie's heart was pounding so hard that she was sure it showed through her shirt. She looked down at Princess Em, who winked. It appeared Liz wasn't the only one running a side gig matchmaking service.

"Reynolds?"

Maggie felt like that Gumby character. Or a bowl of Jell-O. She was debating which while she tried to breathe. Either way, she felt warm all over. *Calling him Coop.* It seemed like an invitation to other things.

"You taking a nap in there, Maggie?"

The lack of *Reynolds* moniker snapped her out of it. "Okay. Sure. Coop it is."

"Well, that's settled, then." He picked up a brown bag Maggie hadn't noticed until now. "I brought ice cream."

Emily squealed and ran to the kitchen.

Maggie turned to follow, but he grabbed her arm. "Say it. Like you mean it, Reynolds." He closed the gap between them, and she thought to say something about his constant use of her last name, except she'd already decided she liked it.

She looked up. The attraction between them couldn't be mistaken. "Okay. Mr. Coop."

He burst out laughing again and closed the door behind them. Turning, his right hand resting lightly against her lower back, he gently ushered her to the kitchen.

CHAPTER TEN

Liz Courts Maggie

Liz sat at a corner table in the deli she and Maggie had gone to for years. Modest prices, great sandwiches and salads, beer and wine, and geographically close enough for both of them to grab a bite and not be tied up in case they had other obligations.

Jake had the kids. She smiled to herself, knowing they'd run circles around him and also knowing he'd keep up. Since Jake finally sanctioned her attempt at a holiday match between Maggie and Coop, Liz needed some time with her best friend to move things along. That kind of "visit" required adult alone time.

Liz had taken the liberty of ordering a half baguette with butter—lots of butter. She was dusting crumbs off her shirt when she spotted her best friend at the deli's sign-in sheet. "Mags. Over here."

Maggie returned a wave and started weaving her way between the crowded tables. Liz took a sip of her zero-alcohol beer, then stood up to pull her friend into a hug. "You look great, Mags. I guess that means the kids are a good group this year. Oh, and the administration isn't implementing some impossible new program to fix something that isn't wrong?"

"My students are wonderful. I'll tell you about the current assignment and all my ideas as soon as we order."

They settled into their chairs. Liz watched her friend closely as Maggie tugged off her blazer and tucked her purse at her feet under the table. She pushed the board with the bread across the table.

"Here, I was starved and figured nothing beats bread and butter for an opener."

"Yum. Sourdough. And cold butter. Perfect. It's like reenacting our first year in the apartment over the Take & Bake Pizza. Except then, baguettes and tub margarine were about all we *could* afford to eat."

"Right? Long time ago, best friend. Long time ago."

Maggie counted on her fingers. "Nineteen years. Oh my God, Liz. This is almost worse than a high school reunion." Liz saw Maggie glance at the pale liquid in her glass. "What're you drinking?"

"Zero-beer. But Jake has the kids if you want to get stupid." Liz raised her hand to get the waiter's attention, noticing that Maggie had broken into a big grin. "And what's so funny?"

"Oh, just thinking of the two of us, the one night a week that we put on the calendar to get blotto but then chickened out. I guess that's a good thing, seeing as how I messed up my life enough sober."

"Come on. You hit a rough patch." Liz realized that her comment didn't match the facts. It was a bit like comparing the burning of Rome to a beach bonfire. "I'm sorry, that's not a very apt description of what you've been through. To think I was your Maid of Honor when you married that creep."

"Hey, it's not like you set me up with him. And don't be sorry. I wouldn't have come out the other side of that marriage without you and Jake. Who else takes in a debunked lawyer and her belongings when her estranged husband wants to kill her? I mean, seriously."

Liz hurt for her best friend–godmother to Annie. It had been Maggie that made Liz go on that first date with Jake. She nibbled at her bread and changed the subject. "But *you,* dear friend, did set me up. What did you say to me that night?"

"What night?" Maggie stared at her from across the table, lowering her menu.

"The then-unpublished-Lizzie-Callahan-goes-out-with-Jake-Willis night. The uber-successful publisher, about-the-book night? The night I broke your best shoes."

"Oh, yeah. My ultimate thrift store find. Buried in the back, next to a collection of old army boots, those fantastic slingback Jimmy Choo's."

"Maybe God put them there for you to find. I mean, look where the shoes led. Me and Jake." Liz smiled at her old friend.

"And thinking back"—Maggie grinned—"what I said was, 'You are so going, Lizzie. You have to.'"

"That's it. So how about we each have a glass of chardonnay and enjoy some great memories?"

Liz waited as Maggie appeared to be debating the idea of alcohol in the early afternoon, then said, "Okay, I'll consider it a pre-holiday splurge. Chardonnay it is. And I presume we've come far enough that the wine can come out of a bottle instead of a box?"

"Absolutely, positively, definitely." Liz winked when she finished the statement. And in harmony, they shouted out, "Adverb abuse."

The remaining lunch crowd looked over, so Liz shrugged an acknowledgement of their silliness to the group of people still eating and the folks at the deli counter ordering things to go.

***

Maggie remained in awe of Liz. So accomplished, still funny, not a hint of wealth or the fame of being a best-selling author changing the Liz she'd met almost two decades ago. They chatted a lot about the kids, Jake, and the fact that he'd taken the brood off Liz's hands for a day.

Liz brought up Maggie's new school year, the students, other teachers, and Maggie filled in the blanks. It reeked of so much normalcy, she didn't have the heart to mention the letters and calls from Teddy Amato.

She should have known better. Maggie knew better than to try and hide stuff like that from her best friend. Thinking she'd beat Liz to the punch, Maggie took another bite of her grilled chicken breast salad and offered, "I know you're worried about me, Liz, but I'm fine, really I am."

"Bullshit." The out-loud expletive couldn't offend any patrons because the deli had all but emptied out. Just ten minutes earlier, Danny, the deli's owner, had signaled the two old friends could stay a bit longer; he'd even brought the bottle of chardonnay that had filled their first two glasses over to the table. "Again, Mags. I call BS." Liz raised her hand, signaling their waiter. He left his current chore of pulling table cloths off to wad up for laundry and came over. She smiled at the young man gratefully.

"I don't want to keep you here, Tim, but could you please get us two slices of chocolate cake? And then the check. Thanks."

Maggie figured it was the wine; her synapses were slow, and she felt safe. As if she and Liz were in one of their old haunting grounds and nobody could touch them. Nobody except Teddy Amato, maybe.

Liz poured out the rest of the wine evenly between their two glasses. Tim showed up with two slices of cake that held enough calories in a single bite to form a pound of body fat. At the same time, with their mutual rejection of doggie boxes, he cleared their plates.

Liz put the cake slices in front of each of them, picked up a fork, and issued a challenge. "Okay, friend. I'm still convinced something is off kilter with you, but one bite each, and then you tell me about babysitting for Nick Cooper."

There was no escaping Liz's scrutiny, and Maggie had no real qualms about discussing her new neighbor. In fact, she'd be remiss if she didn't call Liz out on the "why" of Nick's out-of-the-blue babysitting request. "You mean the neighbor you're trying to set me up with?"

Liz balked, but only a little. She looked across the table at Maggie and shrugged, then took another bite of cake. "So? Maybe I did. That doesn't mean you shouldn't help him out with Emily."

That was true enough. "Okay." Maggie paused, knowing to do so was killing Liz. "I like him, he seems nice, and based on Jake's criteria for editors, he has to be smart." Hearing herself talk about the man made her smile. "His daughter, Emily, is a kick." She felt her face redden under the spotlight of Liz 's stare. Maggie knew she was only a heartbeat away from Liz busting her on the feelings she was beginning to have for Nick Cooper.

"Ah-ha." Liz didn't explain her pronouncement.

Watching Liz's unspoken thoughts register in her expression, Maggie decided to go on the offense. "Don't you go thinking you've had a big success with your annual Happily Ever After set-up. There's not even a hint of anything between us." A lie. "He's a nice man, I've helped him with babysitting one time, his daughter is charming and way too clever, and that's about it."

"You're as red as one of the eight original colors in a crayon box, Mags. Which registers as you're full of you-know-what. And I write HEAs, lest you forget." She took another bite of cake, then asked, "Has he kissed you?"

"Whoa. Slow the Sam Hill down." Maggie picked up her wine glass, intending to slam back the rest of its contents, but took a deep breath instead, setting the glass back down. She needed to save some of it for when she revealed the letters and threatening phone calls. "Okay, I might be attracted to him, but I've no idea how he feels about me, and come on, his wife hasn't been gone two years."

"Do you think because my Jake mourned Samantha for almost nine years before he fell for me that there's some kind of timeline on grief? You know better than that. Jake and I have noticed a huge difference in Nick the last seven months or so, especially his decision to sell the apartment he and Meg lived in forever and move. You don't lose your past; you learn to live with it, and that's what Nick is doing now. And not just because he needs to for Emily's sake, but because he wants to." Liz reached across the table and squeezed Maggie's hand. "You could be part of that, Mags."

Maggie had never doubted her friend's insights, and she'd long learned the impossibility of getting her off track once she honed in on something, so she offered, "I guess he likes me a little."

Liz laughed out loud. "And how have you come to this monumental conclusion?"

Maggie measured how to respond carefully. Liz "capital-L loved" people connecting, particularly when she was responsible. "There's a tension between us, you know, like when we're two inches apart or five feet away, like a magnetic field. I'm trying to stay away from those moments."

"Why?" Liz didn't let up, her gaze intense. "Why would you want to stop this from happening? You like him, and it sounds like he likes you, so is it Emily?"

"No, no, I don't think so. Em's great. She's like an old soul in a seven-year-old's body."

"I guess that shouldn't come as a surprise. She lost her mother at five. Some kids just understand that they have to take control of their lives, even in a sad world."

"I guess that's true." Maggie took another bite of cake. "He's a little regimented, though."

"Really? Well, they do say opposites attract."

"Maybe." Maggie smiled. There was no point in arguing Liz's inference. "But did you know that Nick has a one-inch-thick three-ring binder chock-full of babysitting rules? I mean, it's outlined and everything. I practically had to put my hand on it and swear to follow the damn thing to the letter."

Liz had chosen that moment to swallow from her water glass, with the consequence being a snort accompanied by a channel of water shooting halfway across the table. This time, it was Maggie who burst out laughing.

Liz dabbed at her shirt and face with the napkin. "Well, serious now—there is one test as to whether he likes you for sure."

"And that would be?" Maggie reached for her water glass, still intent on saving the last of her wine for the big reveal.

"He says it's okay for you to call him Coop."

Maggie's turn: she choked on the water going down her throat and promptly developed the hiccups.

***

After a few minutes of Maggie holding her breath and the two of them mopping up the table with their napkins, Liz noticed a hint of darkness behind Maggie's eyes. She'd been there before with her best friend and knew the signs. Something bad was undercutting Maggie's shot at happiness, and Liz intended to find out what it was.

"This has been fun, Mags. But I just watched a cloud gather over your head. You can't hide it from me, and you know it. So, the truth. Now. I'm not leaving here without it." Liz watched her friend's features for subtle changes. Maggie's eyes were surveying the room, and she seemed to be shrinking into herself. Liz had only known Maggie to react in this way when she'd suffered at the hands of her husband.

"If I didn't know better, Mags, I'd say Ricky has come back from the dead." Liz was glad to have saved half of her second glass of wine and reached for it, waiting on a reply.

"Close enough." Maggie looked up from the last bite of cake on her plate. "Teddy found me."

"Holy shit." She set her wine glass down in the space where her plate used to be and folded her napkin with a precision that meant she was all ears. "What the hell?"

CHAPTER ELEVEN

Roses

He'd picked up the roses in the Trader Joe's on Grand at Clinton. Safer to buy at a big and busy store than to use a florist. Cheaper too. Two dozen. Teddy figured that would do it.

When their mom died, Teddy moved into the house. He and Ricky had both owned it, but Ricky was still married to Maggie the Lawyer then. The place was a mess on account of their mom keeping *everything*.

But there was beauty in that too.

He didn't have to look far for what he needed, and sure enough, he found some vases under the sink. He picked a tall one that looked like it came from a flower shop. Probably did, and he'd bet it was from his mom's funeral. He sure had no memory of his father ever bringing flowers. Nope, old Dad didn't have to sweeten up Mom for anything. He'd always gotten what he wanted with his fists.

"And this is some poetic justice," he commented aloud to himself in the big kitchen. Maybe that wasn't the phrase; he didn't care. What mattered was the vase had been for his mom's funeral, and soon, it would signify Maggie-Bitch's end. He held the vase up and looked for chips or cracks.

Teddy had finished the note earlier that day. It was a lot of work. He had to make it so nothing could be tracked to him. Like on the cop shows, when they followed some computer address and nailed somebody for being stupid. He wasn't going to be stupid. He wasn't getting caught because of some chipped letter on a keyboard or something.

Everybody did it. Used words and letters from magazines and newspapers to write kidnap notes, threats, and stuff. Doing it any other way would be stupid. Teddy knew that the same people who could figure out computer addresses and stuff could also match handwriting.

Ricky would have had some good ideas on how to do it, but then Ricky wasn't here. Because the bitch put him away, and putting his brother behind bars was why he was dead, and that was why Teddy had to keep the promise.

The boyhood promised to watch each other's back.

To get even if someone fucked one or the other of them over.

This house was where Ricky came to live when bitch-Reynolds had kicked him out. She served him with divorce papers here too.

It was kind of dangerous that they'd lived at the same address on account of the side hustle—the drugs—but that was what brothers did for each other. Especially Teddy, on account of Ricky being three years younger.

Teddy had long been pushing drugs for Jocko and Mel, childhood buddies. And that was where, eventually, Ricky came in. The band worked as a front. It was easy because they were always moving equipment around and traveling in and out of the state, looking all normal rock-and-roll-shit-like. Stashing a pound of coke or meth in a speaker was a piece of cake.

It had been working good for almost two years, and then Ricky's wife got suspicious. Okay, the band was getting more well-known, the gigs getting more attention, but even if Ricky had told him they were going to have to stop the trafficking, the crap that came down was all her fault. She could change her name back to Maggie Reynolds a hundred times, and it wouldn't fix anything.

Teddy stared at the ceiling, the clippers in his hand. He'd thought about it a lot, but no matter how hard he tried, he couldn't think of a reason his brother had married the chick. A super-skinny lawyer with no real tits and freak-of-nature tall for a woman.

To Teddy's thinking, none of the bad shit would have happened if Maggie hadn't filed for divorce. So, it was all her fault. All of it.

Still, Teddy had hope when Maggie Reynolds "Should-still-have-been-Amato" had shown up at the first hearing. They were nice to each other, and Ricky told Teddy he was even thinking they'd get back together. She got him out on bail that day, but then she'd acted like Ricky was the kiss of death.

She couldn't be Ricky's lawyer anymore because of something called conflict of interest. Worse, she'd joined up with the effing feds, and because of stuff she said, the District Attorney had added charges about Ricky beating Maggie up, and also the thing about sex with a seventeen-year-old. Ricky had been sleeping with some band rat and had broken her jaw on account of her snorting up some of his personal stash without asking. Plus, she was something like seventeen and three-hundred-and-forty days old. And even that wouldn't bring in the feds, except Ricky had taken her on a road trip out of state.

"I warned you, Ricky." Teddy's voice sounded hollow alone in the big house. He pretended Ricky was sitting in the old green recliner, drinking a beer. "I said you can't knock a chick like Maggie around. She'll get all uppity about it and, bam, you get charged with a crime." Teddy felt like it should be legal to hit a bitch like Maggie, but he also understood it was a crime.

And Ricky was hopeless. He was as much addicted to chicks as he was to coke. He'd beat up the women he'd been with just like their old man had done. "You couldn't cool it for a little while, Ricky? I mean, you were out on bail, for crap's sake."

They'd arrested Ricky a second time despite Maggie showing up and fixing stuff at that first hearing. And it was different that time. The dickhead judge wouldn't set bail. Ricky went to trial, and the jury found him guilty of a bunch of stuff.

Teddy slammed the clippers down and took several deep breaths. Remembering shit fueled his anger. Ricky was murdered, and that was why Teddy was standing alone in his dead mom's house, looking at the pieced-together note.

RoSes *arE* red,
*Your **eyes** a*re blue,
Prepare to be dead,
Ha, ha, Fuck *You.*

These roses were a practice run, and he figured on buying two dozen more when the time was right. But first, a few more letters and some calls, then, of course, the roses, and his final goal, Maggie Reynolds Amato herself.

He'd blown the first few letters, having addressed these to M. Amato instead of Reynolds. And once he got the apartment number right, his access to her apartment building had been easy. He wasn't worried about his plan because Benny Di Blasi and he went from kindergarten to the eighth grade together at St. Francis of Assisi Parish School. It was pretty cool—and to Teddy, just one more sign that he was doing the right thing—that Benny worked a couple of nights a week as the doorman in bitch-Maggie's building. He substituted in a rotation for the two regular guys. Like, nobody could work twelve hours a day, seven days a week forever, right?

It was a drag that it cost him fifty bucks every time Benny let him pass and go up the elevator, but this was going to be so worth it.

Fate. Nothing but fate. Especially taking into account her moving a couple of times in the last few years.

Teddy looked at his practice roses. He clipped a few more leaves off, another stem, studying his first attempt. He was getting better at it, and soon—it would be soon—Maggie would be in his possession. And it was all going to be worth it.

CHAPTER TWELVE

Maggie & Coop

Since lunch with Liz, Maggie had felt better about one thing: the possibility of a relationship with Nick "Coop" Cooper. That was ridiculous, his nickname and surname running together like that, but she liked that she'd been given the green light to call him Coop, like people who he'd known and loved for a long time. It spurred a few fantasies about the man.

Okay, a lot of fantasies.

She was anxious to see him again. But now, Coop had disappeared. She'd had the courage to knock on the door twice in the last week. Both times, she met the longstanding babysitter, saw Emily briefly, and returned to her apartment without any information on his status. She also hadn't been alone with Emily either time, or she might have found out what her father was up to.

He was working, of course. There were a lot of publishing details heading into the Christmas season that would put pressure on any editor. But knowing this didn't make her feel any better.

She was so sure of an attraction between them. The tension had been there, and now she wanted his help. Liz had suggested that Maggie tell Coop everything about her past, including the threat from Teddy Amato. Liz also wanted her to go to the police.

Maggie disagreed. At least about the police. Teddy was a foul-mouthed thug, all talk, no action—she hoped. And what did she have as evidence? A few phone threats that only she heard and a handful of letters, no return address, unsigned.

Still, in the time between their lunch and now, Liz's words had hounded Maggie, so worrying about it today was easy. It was Saturday, and she had nothing to keep her busy; even the deadline for her students' story drafts wasn't until next Friday. So, she'd completed a thorough and therapeutic cleaning of the apartment and sent off a grocery order online. The latter was a clever way to have a reason to be sitting around all day. With everything done, there was nothing left but to wear a path from the front door to the kitchen bar counter and back.

"Hey, Reynolds. You in there?" The question was accompanied by the buzz of her doorbell and pounding on the door.

Coop.

Maggie waited a beat, although, in truth, she could barely breathe. "Who?"

"Come on, neighbor. It's Coop."

She opened her door and, straight-faced, said, "I don't know a Coop."

"You do. Remember, we voted. It was unanimous." Instead of walking past her when he came through the door, Coop stopped, invading her space, and she didn't care. "I'm hoping you missed me, Reynolds."

"Did you go somewhere?" The nerve endings in her hands and feet sent rapid-fire signals up her limbs that left a fuzzy feeling below her waist and made her mind feel numb.

"I was working, Reynolds. I know you dropped by because Emily made a point of telling me"—he grinned—"about *both* times."

"Well, it wasn't to see you, that's for sure. I was checking on Emily."

He moved an inch closer. Another few centimeters and her breasts would brush up against his shirt. She braved a look at his face. The grin was still there, and the dimples on either side of his mouth were in full force. Given her height, she didn't have to stretch her neck to evaluate his expression, and his shirt was undone enough that she could see his Adam's apple and the ridge of both clavicle bones. Too damned sexy. How was it that he loved only one woman, that he'd steered clear of relationships after his wife died? It seemed impossible, but those facts reinforced her hope that he liked her.

And why was he here now? Probably not for her. She'd wager Emily needed a babysitter.

She felt it coming, the sneeze, and quickly turned her head. "Achoo." Her sleeve took the brunt.

"Bless you."

"Thanks."

"Did you catch Emily's cold? I'm so sorry."

"No. No cold. I cleaned house all morning. It's probably dust, bleach, all those healthy chemicals it takes for the infamous 'spit shine.'"

Coop put his hands on her shoulders, studying her. The scrutiny of his inspection caused a core meltdown and left her uncertain on her feet.

"You sure you're not sick? I'd feel terrible if you got sick helping me out."

"Nick, it's noth…"

"Coop, Reynolds. Please?"

Well, and what was he going to call her? Reynolds forever? Oh, hell. She liked it. It made her feel special. She was sure he didn't call Liz, Willis, or anyone else in that fashion. At least she chose to see it that way.

He looked over her shoulder without changing his position. "Where's the school work?"

"I'm caught up. Well, until end of next week, anyway. That's when the kids should turn in the final draft of their Christmas assignment."

"Hmm. Hey, it does smell clean in here. I didn't know you were such a great housekeeper."

Who was this man? He'd gone from the calm, quiet, almost reticent gentleman, widower dad-person to a silly boy. She voiced her observation, "Who are you?" and dared a direct look.

Bad idea. Totally toast.

His deep laugh sent her further over the edge. "I know. I've been out of touch, but last week was officially hell week as far as editing went. I spent three nights at the office and the other four—" He stared up at her ceiling as if trying to calculate how he'd spent his time for those other four days. "I must have been there until two or three a.m. the other nights." He released her arms, and suddenly, she missed the touch. "Let's sit."

"Fine."

"You sure you're okay? I don't have much to go on in terms of comparison to how you looked a year, or even two months ago, but you look pretty good now."

Was that a compliment? Maggie didn't respond.

"Damn, that sounded terrible. But you do—look great."

She sat down on one end of the couch and pulled her knee up, leaning into the cushions on her left side, watching as he sat at the other end. Maggie used the time he took to situate himself to assess his appearance. So different from the business attire—all she'd really seen him in—and now, his denim shirt was tucked into regular old button-fly jeans, and he wore tennies instead of expensive Italian shoes. Maggie was imagining him with his shirt off, a button undone on his jeans and…

"I was speaking with Jake Willis in the office the other day," Coop said, "and he said something, I can't remember what exactly— I think it was a mystery we were considering—but it reminded me about the letter I gave you, the weird one addressed wrong. And I remembered the other few I gave back to the post office, and it hit me. Something must be going on in your life, and I forgot to follow up."

"You got other letters?"

"Yes."

"Weird. Well, it's no big deal."

"Isn't it?"

"Nope. Pinky lock."

"And you don't want to share? Because maybe I could help."

How, Nick, Coop, Cooper? How do I tell you about the phone calls? Do I let you read my letters? Maggie hadn't even told Liz about the most recent letter slipped under her door a day after their lunch. She'd promised herself and Liz she'd tell Coop. But sitting here, in broad daylight, it felt like she'd blown things out of proportion. "It's nothing. Really. Thanks, though." He looked a bit stricken, and she felt compelled to remedy any bad feelings he had from her response. "How's Emily?"

"Okay, I'll change the subject. For now. Emily's great. Loves school. Misses you, though."

"She does?"

"Yep. Sometimes I get the feeling she's trying to set me up with you."

In my dreams, Coop. "She's a little girl who lost her mom. It's natural that she'd try and rope you into some relationship."

"I'm not sure I'd feel roped, Reynolds." He caught her looking, and she couldn't escape his gaze. The intensity in his expression catapulted the color in his eyes from a mere blue to something more like that blue contrast that happened against a setting sun, deepening as each minute passed until twilight gave way to nighttime.

"Coop, is something wrong? I mean, why *are* you here?"

"Simple. Here to see you."

"Right."

"Not kidding. You make me laugh."

"Is that because I'm funny, or because I end up being comical by accident, like walking into walls and things?"

His laughter did what it had before: created that fuzzy feeling from her toes up to her forehead. She wasn't sure what to do but figured it was bad form to jump his bones.

"You see?" he said. "No, it's not just you're accident-prone, but also…"

She cut him off. "Me, accident-prone?"

He was about to say something, but there was a tap at the door. They both turned and watched an envelope get shoved through the narrow gap between the bottom of the door and the hardwood floor. Maggie was up, had the envelope retrieved, and barely gave it a sideways glance.

Coop was there too, but he pulled open the door and looked up and down, then ran toward the elevator. "Dammit." He disappeared when he turned down another hall that led to the stairs but came back still looking over his shoulder.

"I missed him." His face was set with a concerned look. It took Maggie by surprise. He closed the door behind him and flipped the deadbolt. "Hey, that looks a lot like the envelopes I gave you awhile back."

"Indeed."

"This is serious, Reynolds. Someone left that for you, and whether it was the person who wrote it or a lacky, they know where you live."

"No, not really." Maggie's brain raced for a reason to receive the weird letters in a way that wasn't a threat. She stuffed the envelope in her back pocket. "It's a game an old friend and I play. I didn't say anything more about it to you because it's so stupid. We create clues from books we've read, math puzzles for directions, and stuff like that. When one of us gets the answer, the loser buys lunch. It's a bit like that game, you know, some professor with a wrench in the conservatory? It takes a couple of months."

"Sounds intriguing." He didn't look convinced.

Maggie pushed through the immediate thought to tell him everything. She couldn't. If there was something between them, it was too new, and she didn't want to lose it by dragging in her past. She'd managed Ricky Amato and survived, and she'd manage whatever it was Teddy had up his sleeve as well.

"God, look at the time." A ridiculous attempt at throwing him out, she stood, knowing she didn't want him to go.

"Are you throwing me out?"

"I hate to, I do." She thought he looked resigned to her decision to cut off a discussion that was likely to bring them closer to one another.

"I think you're hiding something from me. I get it, sort of. This is new." He motioned to her and back to himself. "And trust is an issue. But I'm not going away." He reached for the envelope in her back pocket, bringing them inches apart again, but she dodged the grab. "And I'm here if you need help."

"Thanks, but like I said. It's a game."

He didn't budge, and Maggie thought the heat between them must be palpable. Her desire for him was screaming from places on her body he couldn't hear. *Just tell him, Maggie. Let him help you get out of* this. It was Liz's voice, her words that pushed Maggie to say yes to Coop, maybe getting closer to him. He was physically near enough to fold her into his arms and shield her against the madness that had consumed her life for the Ricky years. She just couldn't. Her self-esteem had been rebuilt from the ground up, and she wasn't sure how to let anyone in without chipping away at it somehow.

"I'll wait, Reynolds. I'll wait. But if anything happens to you because you're afraid to share—"

He didn't finish the sentence. And she knew it wasn't a threat. At least it didn't feel like one. "Honest. It has nothing to do with you, Coop. And the letter is just what I said. Part of a long-playing game between a friend and colleague. It's like a scavenger hunt of sorts. It's not worth even trying to explain the rules."

All of it was a bald-faced lie. She was going to let him walk out of her apartment, suspecting that lying to Coop was against his book of rules. That being deceitful was unforgivable, certainly for an adult friend. Perhaps the pressure wasn't as great for little seven-year-old girls.

"Okay. You know you can't keep your secrets forever, right?"

"I get that. There's not much to tell. And even if there was? Maybe you can listen, but you can't edit my past any more than I can change yours." The intense concern in his eyes, the way he was studying her, probably gauging whether she was telling the truth. His hand came up to her face. Hair had fallen over her eyes again, and he pushed it back behind an ear, brushing her cheek with his thumb in the process. The touch sent shivers from the place of his caress, following the nerve endings down her neck, her back, into both arms and down her spine, settling as a ball of heat at her core.

She wanted him to kiss her, to take her face in both hands and start slow, with a light kiss on her lips, then deeper, drawing her in and pulling her down onto the sofa. She wanted all of what he promised with the look that remained on his face, unwavering.

Coop did kiss her. Just as she'd been imagining. A soft touch of their lips that she could swear sent sparks in the air. He lingered a moment longer, his forehead against hers. "I'll see you tomorrow. Think about what I said."

He turned and walked out the door without another word.

Her body ached, but her mind wouldn't allow him to help her, and Maggie wouldn't dare involve him and Emily. Teddy Amato was dangerous.

The position she was in was hers to manage.

Maggie had known it for years, known that despite all the past chapters of her life she managed to close, there was some kind of freaking epilogue that waited. She was in it now.

Moving despite the weakness that consumed her from being so close to Coop, she methodically secured all the locks on her door.

***

She'd poured herself a glass of wine, and apparently, she'd eaten something because a plate sat on the coffee table. Cracker crumbs and a piece of cheese occupied the Fiesta ware, the leftovers looking bereft against the bold yellow color. Maggie had no idea how long she'd been sitting there, but the apartment was dark except for the nightlight that came on automatically in the kitchen.

Her eyes were puffy because she'd been crying.

The damned letter, a piece of paper that seemed to herald from hell itself, sat beside her on the couch.

Nothing Teddy put in the letter was any different, except his tone was angrier. He'd used the word bitch about eight times. It was almost funny that he'd managed to cut out enough b-i-t-c-h letters from magazines, newspapers, and the like to threaten her again and again.

Not that Teddy had ever been articulate, but it was obviously harder to complete sentences or be grammatically correct when pasting together cut-out letters into a document threatening someone's life.

Exhausted and numb, she stood and stretched, leaving everything as it was, and forced herself to crawl into bed.

The only redeeming thing from the evening? The kiss. The *I want you* look in Coop's eyes. And he said he'd see her tomorrow, so she could re-think asking for his help. "Yikes." She sat bolt upright in bed as her daily calendar flashed before her eyes. Of course she'd see him tomorrow. She'd agreed to babysit Emily again.

***

Maggie woke up feeling excited. She had already had one cup of coffee, made the bed, and, after showering, started a load of laundry.

She thought about making something for lunch and remembered once again she was babysitting Emily. From past experience, Coop would have plenty of food to fatten the two of them up while he was working. All of the Christmas book deadlines had come and gone, and with the finished products expected back from printers any minute, Coop had made it clear: if she could, he needed her most weekends up until release dates, of which many would be Thanksgiving.

It was fine with her. It made for three weeks in which she'd see him at least in her care of Emily. Maggie had come to love Emily.

She caught a glance of herself in the hall mirror and wondered, was she prepared to make that same admission about Emily's father?

It was almost ten; time to go. With one last look in the mirror, reassured that she didn't look like a liar, nor that she'd had a crying jag after he left last night, she reached for her full-of-stuff leather bag in the hall closet.

The doorbell buzzed, and she jumped.

"Who is it?" No answer. Opening the peephole, she saw nobody. Another letter? No, the threats from Teddy came under the door. It must be Emily. Coop could be standing in his doorway, letting her cross over to make sure Maggie was on time.

She threw open the door to hug her young friend.

Instead, two dozen red roses with a card stuffed into the flowers sat before her, an incarnation of evil itself.

She knew in an instant these weren't from a florist. There was no little plastic stick to hold up the card, and the flowers were smashed in the vase without a florist's touch. At least one failing blossom flopped limp over the lip of the vase.

She'd been wrong. Liz was right. Maggie wanted Coop to know. To tell him everything. Anything he was willing to hear.

Well, she'd blown that.

The past had become the present. Teddy was the equivalent of Ricky in too many ways to count. She swooped up the vase and triple-locked the door. Leaving the roses on the entry table, she sat on the sofa and started to cry.

"Shit, shit, shit, damn it—" She swiped the tears away before they became a torrent and, after running to the bathroom, splashed water on her face. Like some kind of quick change for a model heading back to the runway, she patted a little concealer around her eyes, popped in a couple squirts of eyedrops, and re-did her eyeliner. A touch of bronze blush to cover up red cheeks, and she would still be on time. Lucky for her, she'd never been one for a lot of makeup.

What about the roses?

She stacked her shoes and boots on top of one another in the hall closet and set the vase of blooms and the unread note inside. She closed the closet door. *Out of sight, out of mind?* Maggie couldn't remember where the phrase came from, but she hoped it was true. Opening her front door, she stepped out just as Emily came flying across the hall and into her arms. "Mags, you'll be late. Come on. Daddy has to get going."

Coop waved from the door and disappeared back inside. By the time she and Emily crossed the threshold, he was ready to go.

"Reynolds, thanks. I appreciate your help."

"You know I love sitting with Emily."

Emily had dashed down the hall for something.

"Remember what I said last night. I do want to develop trust with you, convince you to trust me. Just a thought." Coop sounded so matter-of-fact, and yet he leaned in, his look intense. He smelled of that woodsy aftershave, and once again, she wanted him to fold her into his arms.

Instead, she found the courage to smile at him. "I got it. Thanks."

"Emily Rose?" he called out. No answer. "I'm leaving. You behave for Maggie."

Emily appeared pink-cheeked with a handful of stuffed animals. "I will, Daddy."

Coop smiled at his daughter and gave Maggie a quick grin. "See *you* this afternoon, Reynolds." The door closed behind him, and knowing he'd wait on the other side of the door until he heard the sound, she slid and turned the locks in place.

CHAPTER THIRTEEN

Jake & Coop

Jake nursed a light beer, read a few quick texts from Liz—she'd already begun her Thanksgiving quests—and sent a few replies. He relinquished the control he didn't really have, and Liz being a whirlwind never bruised his ego.

Jake focused on the room and watched for his friend. He saw Coop get waved in and smiled as Coop walked toward him. Liz was right about one thing: Coop would be a catch for any woman.

Today, though, Jake just wanted to touch base. Of course, they could chat in the office, but that wasn't the place to judge how Coop was handling the mundane—regular old living stuff, like losing Meg. Something Jake understood, the moving on from grief.

Jake shoved images of his first wife, Sam, and 9-11 out of his mind. Twenty-two memorials under his belt, and that day could still grab him out of a happy sleep and toss him into a nightmare. He pushed his chair back and stood as his best editor approached. Grabbing Coop's hand, Jake pulled him into a bear hug. "Hey, bud. You look good."

"Considering everything, I *am* good."

Coop's voice didn't waver, and Jake took it as a good sign. He had additional reasons to invite his colleague and friend to lunch. He called it "The Lizzie Directive."

"It's not just how you're doing after losing your wife, Coop. You know I've been there. I want to know how you're *really* doing."

"I'm sorry," Coop said. "I know I sounded a bit testy. I appreciate your asking and the lunch invite. You, by the way, look pretty good for an old man."

Jake laughed and stood back, studying his friend a little more closely. The difference in their ages was significant, but they had too much in common for that to be an issue. Sure, in a few more years, it was unlikely Jake would keep beating Coop at tennis, but he'd face that crap when it happened.

They settled into their chairs, and the waiter took Coop's drink order. Coop studied his menu for a few seconds, then set it aside and smiled. "Thanks again for your help with that last book edit. It's a good story, a page-turner, at least it was for me. I'm hoping for a bestseller but..."

Jake interrupted, "*We're* hoping for a bestseller."

"I just couldn't seem to fix the little things. Your few edits and plot suggestions were critical."

The tone of respect in Coop's voice was real, and Jake nodded his appreciation. "Yeah, well, little things can make a big difference. I did another read a week ago. You were right. It's a book that warrants a hefty first print. Your writer, once again, didn't disappoint."

Coop's drink arrived, a club soda with lime, and he took a gulp. "I'm always amazed at the process, even after all these years."

"It's a solid story, Nick. And there's nothing like the added element of murder and mayhem to make it a great summer read."

Coop looked up, definitely surprised at the use of his birth name. "And you're calling me Nick, why? Am I getting fired or something?"

"No."

"Moved to the LA branch?"

"No." Jake signaled for the waiter so they could give their orders. Not only was he hungry, but he needed to give Coop a heads-up on Liz's Christmas shenanigans. They'd both feel better fortified with food. Once their orders were headed toward the kitchen, and after covering all the bases about Emily, school, etc., Jake figured he might as well jump in. "It's about Lizzie."

"My god. She's not sick, is she?"

"No, Lizzie's fine." Jake sipped his beer. "And it's not just about Liz. I'm afraid your name keeps coming up."

"You're not making much sense."

"Give me a minute—here's our food."

With the niceties exchanged and the waiter convinced after much discussion that Jake and Coop really didn't need anything else, they were left alone to talk. It was late in the lunch hour, and the crowded room had emptied considerably.

After a few bites of his salad, Jake looked up to see Coop waiting. Anticipating whatever was going on.

"You know of Lizzie's quirky holiday matchmaking?" Jake asked.

"Sure. She's a legend."

Jake waited. Coop was too smart to miss the connection.

"Shit."

Jake muffled his bark of laughter at Coop's realization.

"Me?" Coop said.

"You," Jake confirmed.

"Oh, no. No, no. She's got to stop thinking she can bring people together into some sunset-and-crashing-waves-on-the-beach HEA."

"Yeah, well, that would be like getting her to stop writing books."

Coop reached for a French fry on his plate. He didn't look up and just kept running the fry around a smaller potato slice. He seemed to be circling the wagons. "Geeze, has Liz ever considered that we guys are capable of finding the right person for ourselves?"

"Nope, don't think so."

"Well, go home and tell her no. I don't care if it takes a knock-down, drag-out fight. Tell her no. Flat out. A big negative. Negatory. Absolutely not. I'm not doing this."

"I get it. But consider this: her success rate is like ninety percent."

"Sure, out of how many—three tries?"

"Nope. More like eight."

"And I'm supposed to be another statistic?"

Jake smiled, but not because of his friend's frustration. Sitting across from Coop now, it struck: Liz was right. "You know her already."

"I don't."

"Yeah. You do."

"Jake, who the fu…"

"Hold on, Coop." Interrupting, Jake wanted his friend to process the possibilities. "You're upset. But think of it this way: eventually, whether you like it or not, the woman is going to be somewhere you are unless, of course, you plan to spend this upcoming holiday season without us?"

"Well, yeah, maybe, if it means getting me suckered into something."

"Emily would kill you."

"I know. Of course I'll be there," Coop said. "You know I've been trying to get back into things. But you said I *know* Liz's planned meet-cute?"

"Sort of."

"Come on, what's sort of? The few times I've been at your house for one of Lizzie's Friday wine-and-pizza nights, there were two single women there. Nice, pretty, articulate, but nothing that attracted me or made me want to take it a step further."

"Well, it's not one of them," Jake said.

"Okay. I give. If I met this person through you and Lizzie, and if I had any interest, I would remember. Hell, I would have *told* you about her."

"See, that's the thing about Lizzie's schemes. She doesn't expect you to say anything about this girl—sorry, woman—because that's what makes her antics so successful."

Coop returned to staring at his food. He started eating his open-faced mushroom burger. After a few bites, he said, "This is delicious. I'd forgotten. We used to come here all the time, remember? You, Lizzie, me, and Meg and…" He stopped and, stretching, looked from the ceiling back to Jake. "God, sometimes I just can't believe she's gone. It'll be okay for days. Lately, I've made it a couple of weeks before the pain hits. Emily and I will get along just fine, life as, you know…" Coop put down his fork but didn't speak. After a few moments, he looked directly at Jake. "It's just so fucking hard."

Jake knew exactly how hard it was.

Numb.

Always, his pain over losing Sam was undercut by her pain—for what she must have gone through that day. He banished the image of the South Tower melting into the ground from his head. For eight years, he'd hidden himself from the world. Eight years until Liz.

Coop looked a little lost. "I'm sorry. I guess I've ruined our casual lunch."

"It's okay. Gave me a chance to ruminate a little on my own. We've known each other way too long to have to explain a brain break or two."

"Brain break? I like that. You okay if I use it sometime? Could be a cryptic margin note."

"It's a Lizzie-ism, but I know she won't mind."

Coop smiled for the first time in ten minutes. "And speaking of Lizzie: who *is* this mystery girl that your matchmaker wife believes I'll fall head-over-heels in love with and whom, apparently, I've already met?"

"Uh, well—" Jake motioned to the waiter, figuring that once he disclosed the information, Coop would want a belt of something.

"Jake, old buddy, I'm waiting here—"

"Maggie Reynolds."

Coop looked down at his food, then back to Jake. By then the waiter had made it to the table, and Coop managed, "Scotch. Neat."

"Yes, sir," the waiter said. "Single or doubl—"

Coop interrupted with, "Just the one, but thanks for asking."

The young waiter turned to Jake, a *You need something, sir?* on his face. Jake was still nursing his beer and responded, "I'm fine, thanks."

Once the waiter left, Coop looked at Jake. "My babysitter? Are you kidding me? My effing babysitter?"

"Come on. That part's mostly coincidental."

"Mostly?"

Jake grinned and opened his hands on either side of his plate, the gesture a kind of *here goes nothing*. "Who helped you find your new apartment?"

The dawning. Coop's face went through a few stages—but the one that stuck was his awareness that Liz had helped Coop find an apartment across the hall from Maggie Reynolds.

"Not exactly a coincidence, Jake. So, your wife knows Maggie as more than just an acquaintance?"

"Maggie's responsible for me taking Liz out. They were roommates and besties, as people say these days." As soon as he said it, Jake felt old, but he continued. "I don't suppose you remember a little eatery, Maggie's Take & Bake Pizza & Rooftop Gardens?"

Coop made a face as if he was running through images of places he knew. "No, pretty odd name. I'd remember."

"Yes, odd, but actually moderately successful, at least the pizza business. Maggie sold it years ago."

Jake could see the light dawning on Coop's face: furrowed brow, chewing on his bottom lip, all as he connected the relationship dots. Maggie was Liz's best friend. Maggie lived in the same apartment building. No, on the *same* floor as Coop and Emily. Across the hall.

Coop's drink arrived. He looked briefly at Jake. "And I'm supposed to accept this whole thing as fate?"

Jake lifted his beer, hoping his old friend wasn't planning on killing his wife. "Coop?" Coop raised his glass as well, and Jake said, "Lizzie *is* fate."

CHAPTER FOURTEEN

Coop's Revelation

Screw the elevator. Nick took the stairs up to the apartment two at a time. He paused on the third landing, not because he was out of breath but because he'd been thinking about Maggie more and more.

Once he reached the fifth floor, he took deep breaths, closed his eyes, and pressed the index and middle fingers of one hand against his wrist. He counted his heart rate for sixty seconds. *You're still alive.* And for the first time in two years, he was beginning to feel like it.

Whatever he thought of Liz's antics, he had to see Maggie one way or the other because she was babysitting his kid. It would help if his daughter liked her. Okay, there'd be no relationship if Emily didn't, so the babysitting gig was good for more than the obvious help Maggie was providing.

Was that using her? He glossed over the possibility in his mind. For the moment, he wondered if his reaction to Maggie had changed, knowing that Liz Willis thought he and she should be together. Admittedly, since the first aid episode in Maggie's apartment, he'd been inventing ways to see her.

He waited in front of the apartment door, feeling stupid for just standing outside his own home. He turned the key in the lock and pushed. Okay, good. Maggie had used the deadbolt and the slider. His key could manage the one but not the slider. That took someone on the inside. He knocked on the door.

Nothing.

He didn't hear footsteps.

Pounding on the door, he called out, "Hey—" He listened. "Reynolds, Em, you in there?" The door was pretty solid, but not so much that one wouldn't hear a loud TV or stereo. He pounded again. The door opened just as his fist came down for another strike, landing a direct, whamming hit on Maggie's cheek and under-eye area.

She toppled backwards, a "Holy bee stings, that hurt" coming out of her mouth. Maggie landed hard—first on her rear end, then, as she further crumpled, she bounced back, knocking her head on the floor.

"Damn, Reynolds, I'm so sorry." Panic-stricken, Nick moved to her side.

"I'm okay." She pushed herself into a sitting position, though Nick thought she looked dazed. Maggie was rubbing her right cheek, and he could see the skin was flushed red.

He strode to the couch, grabbed a big pillow, and, squatting at her side, shoved it behind her. "Crap, are you okay?" She didn't say anything but accepted the presence of the pillow willingly and rested against it. "Your jaw could be broken."

She still didn't speak. In fact, her only comment had been the "holy bee stings" expletive. It wasn't an expression he'd forget, and he was impressed she'd had the wherewithal *not* to swear in front of Emily. Still, it added to his impression she was quirky. Nick reached to feel the back of her head, and she slapped him away. He grabbed her hand, shocked at how cold it felt. Using his other hand, he felt from the top of her head down the back of her skull. He expected the lump but was surprised at its size.

"I'm going to call 911," he said.

"Uh, no, you're not."

He glanced at Maggie. She looked mad but seemed aware of her surroundings. "Hell, yes."

Emily stepped in between them. She looked first from Maggie, then to her dad, and then back to Maggie. "No swearing."

"You're right, Em, I'm sorry." He had lowered his voice, and were the situation not so serious, he would have smiled at her officiousness.

"And Daddy, that 'D' word is a very bad word." Emily looked up at him with big doe eyes.

She didn't know many curse words—he hoped—but on enough occasions, she'd been in the right place at the wrong time. "I'm sorry, sweetheart. We can put quarters in the swear jar tomorrow." She appeared satisfied, so he returned his attention to Maggie.

He refocused on her bruised face, thinking about the lump on the back of her head, and a fierce need to protect the woman on his floor stunned his senses. He was on the verge of mumbling another swear word when it dawned. Shit-squared.

He was falling for his babysitter after all.

***

She was aware of Coop's scrutiny, but Maggie was also watching Emily's face. She didn't seem the least bit satisfied with her father's excuses about the abuse of language. Through a developing mid-haze, Maggie also worried about how Emily was processing the accidental blow Coop had landed.

"It's not too cold out, but do you want me to get you a coat from your apartment?" His question, which Maggie thought was totally off the wall, drew her back to the room; she'd been drifting in and out. At least, she thought that explained the gaps in her thinking.

"Why are you worried about me putting on a coat? It's plenty warm in here." She'd been regrouping, trying to find a graceful way to at least get off the floor. She looked up at Coop, and he seemed terrified. Her eyelid must be swelling up. The expression on his face also suggested she might be showing bruises already.

Maggie had her own scale for injuries. *Been there, done that.* Testing under her eye gently with two fingers, she figured it for a

Class 1 Bruise on that scale. She pressed on the bruise and winced. Her brain fog increased.

Of course, Nick, a.k.a. Coop, didn't know about her life before babysitting. Her mind tried to re-visit his proposal that she put a coat on, but her head had begun to pound. He must have left because now he stood over her with a coat.

It wasn't hers.

"We're going to get this coat on you because you need to be seen by a doctor," he said. "The eye doesn't look good. *And* you hit your head."

"Bull—" Maggie bit her tongue from completing the automatic response. Ms. Emily Rose was still standing there. She wondered how Mr. Nick-Coop-Cooper—the sound of his names in her head made her chuckle—would treat her if his daughter was not in the mix. "Even if I said you *could* take me to an ER, what would you do with Em?"

"I can get you to the ER and make sure you're okay, in good hands, whatever. Then I can take Em to Lizzie and Jake's. They won't mind. She can spend the night. I'll come back, check on you, and get you back to your apartment." He paused and looked closer at her cheek and eye. "Yikes, that's a doozy. I'm so sorry."

He reached behind her head again, and she would have objected, except his fingers felt good against her scalp.

He kept prodding around her skull. "Are you dizzy?" He pulled back and looked at her eyes again. "Seeing stars?"

"Hmm, dizzy, but unless you're a rock star and are keeping that secret from the world, no, no stars." She liked the little half-smile that settled on his face with her comment. "I don't think it was really your fault."

"No?"

"No."

"Well, I was pounding on the door. Maybe I could have shown a little more restraint."

"That could be an admission against interest, Mr. Cooper. And maybe it is your fault." She couldn't help it: she broke into a grin. "So maybe you should worry about lawyer Maggie going all legal on you."

"Sure. I would, but you're not a lawyer, at least not anymore. And you still haven't explained that, but for now, it's not the same thing."

A piece of her past she'd originally figured would never be shared with her totally hot neighbor.

Coop was staring at her, his face a bit of a question mark, or maybe it was just that she was seeing double.

"You're right," Maggie said. "I stand corrected. But could you please help me up and over to my apartment?"

"Nope."

Frustration grabbed at her. She knew her entire face was red now, not just the bruise. "I'm sure nothing's broken. I've got plenty of ice at home…"

"Again, Maggie—you're not going home."

She could give up or make a stink, but her head was really starting to hurt, her eye beginning to blur, and she wondered if maybe that was because of blood. "Okay, I'll sue you later."

"Really?"

"I'm thinking about it."

"You're exasperating."

"Probably." Maggie paused. "I'm also kidding. And at this point, I really don't feel good."

"Damn it, Reynolds. Why'd you put up such a fight?"

She shrugged her shoulders and took a moment to enjoy his arms helping her up and into a chair. Emily had disappeared for a moment but came running out of the hallway and across the living room floor to Maggie's chair. "Here, Mags, it's my SpongeBob blanket. It's so cozy." She laid it across Maggie's lap while Maggie felt herself struggling to stay awake. *What little girl uses a word like cozy?*

She heard snippets of things for a little longer, like Emily being told to pack her SpongeBob back pack with a pair of clean underwear, her PJs, and an extra t-shirt for tomorrow morning. After that, she only remembered closing her eyes.

***

How did I get here? She recognized the green-painted walls and the linoleum floor, but she didn't remember how Coop got her out the door, into the elevator, into his car, or much about the ride to the hospital. Emily had kept leaning forward from the middle of the back seat, pushing against her seat belt and rubbing Maggie's left arm, which had rested on the console between the front seats. She remembered it was a nice car as if she was in a commercial about a high-end vehicle.

Maggie also remembered Coop's deep voice. "Emily, you need to sit back in the seat. I don't want to have to ask for two gurneys when we get there."

And there'd been nervous chatter and endless questions from Emily, some of which registered in Maggie's mind: "Why did you have to pound so hard, Daddy? We were making popcorn, and you know you can't walk away and leave popcorn on the stove," and, "She has to be okay, Dad. Is Maggie going to be okay?"

It felt like forever, yet it seemed like an instant because they were in the ER bay, and people in medical outfits were lifting her out of the car and into a wheelchair. She couldn't recall anything about her purse, but somehow Coop was able to hand the administrative-looking woman with a clipboard, her ID, and insurance cards. She also thought he relayed a short description of how her injury occurred, but she wasn't sure.

Maggie *was* sure of his voice in her ear. "I'll be back after I get Emily to Liz and Jake's." She remembered Emily waving and Coop with a grimace on his face when he leaned in one last time. "When you can, Reynolds, you'll have to tell me why these people seem to know you here and why the admitting nurse looked at me like I'm a monster."

She heard herself say to him, "Long story. I'm sorry."

And in her head, *Shit.* He'd find out for sure now. Her past, the one she'd tried so hard to bury. The multiple trips to an ER, and, many times, this same ER. Black eyes. Bruised ribs. One concussion. The time they had to dig glass out of her shoulder because she'd fallen onto the shards of a broken wine bottle after Ricky smashed it against the counter and then pushed her to the floor. A chronically sprained wrist from the tug-and-pull routine her ex-husband loved best.

And the looks of the people in the ER. The business cards for social services pressed into her hand, the whispers in her ear, "We can get you help, Mrs. Amato." Maggie had all those cards in a drawer. She kept them as a reminder of the past; the size of the stack gave her strength. She'd never thought to correct her hospital records when she'd stopped being Mrs. Amato. Why would she? Ricky was dead, and she'd believed she could stop running.

Now, she was here by accident. She needed to wake up—to make sure they knew the man who'd dropped her off was not another Ricky.

She remembered saying, "He's not Ricky; he's okay," a few times. But she was tired, and she was hurt, and when the nurse covered her with a warm blanket, she closed her eyes.

CHAPTER FIFTEEN

The Willis Rescue

Jake opened the door to Nick and Emily. "Guys, come in. I guess you've had quite a night so far."

"That's an understatement," Nick muttered wearily. "Thanks for agreeing to take Emily."

"If you hadn't asked, I'd have your hide." Coming from out of the hallway that led to the bedrooms, Liz gave her Liz-Willis-sucked-everybody-in smile.

Nick felt a sense of relief as Emily ran into Liz's arms for a big hug.

"Are you okay, Ms. Emily Rose?" Liz said as she cuddled Emily.

"Oh, Mrs. W., it was scary, but Mags was so brave, and Daddy didn't mean to hit her in the face and make her fall down. The doctor said she might have a pin cushion."

It was a simultaneous head snap, like some awkward ballet, as both Jake and Liz turned to stare at Nick.

"I can explain," Nick said. "And it's a concussion, Em. I want to get back to the hospital, so here's the synopsis. When I got back to the apartment, the slide bolt was locked, my standing orders, so I was knocking on the door. I didn't get an answer. I couldn't hear noises inside, so I panicked and started pounding."

Neither Jake nor Liz said a word, waiting patiently, and Emily, as if to confirm Nick's story, nodded her head in a universal yes.

"Reynolds opened the door suddenly," Nick continued. "My fist was up and carried through, smacking her in the face. She fell backwards and hit her head." He took a fortifying breath. "And now she's in the ER. With a suspected light concussion."

"Well, okay, then." Liz leaned in and gave him a hug. "And you *will* want to get back ASAP, so Emily, what say we go down the hall? I've got the other twin bed made up in Annie's room. If you're hungry, we'll think of something to eat, but let's get you settled first."

"Coop?" Liz got his attention. "I think Annie will keep Em from having any reaction to so much drama, so I sort of made an assumptive close that she would stay here with us, at least tonight and longer if you need. We can figure out getting her back to you when you know more about Maggie's condition."

"That would be great. Thanks, Liz. And, Emily?"

"Yes, Daddy."

"You call me if you need anything. I love you."

"Of course you do, Daddy. I love you back, to the moon and stuff. See you later." With a wave, Emily headed down the hall, holding Liz's hand and yammering on about his smacking Maggie in the face.

Jake smiled and, with a gentle shove on Nick's shoulder, motioned him to follow into the den. Nick noticed that Jake had already poured his habitual two-fingers of bourbon, a nightly ritual he'd witnessed firsthand on work visits. He felt awkward about the intrusion.

"I'm sorry. I feel bad about disrupting your evening."

"Nonsense. Emily doesn't need to be dragged around ERs, and you need to focus on, uh, your *babysitter*?"

"Don't start, friend."

"Okay, I'm sorry. I know you're driving, but you want a single belt?"

"I'd love a shot, but better not. I haven't eaten, and I need to get back to the hospital and find out if Reynolds is in for the night or whether I'm going to be able to get her home."

"To your place?"

Nick knew he couldn't keep much from his mentor and friend. But he still wasn't sure what his feelings were toward his neighbor. Maggie got to him, no doubt about it. It was just so damn creepy that Liz Willis knew it first, that she wanted to put them together. Forever.

"It depends. If she's got a concussion or something, I don't think protocol will allow the hospital to release her without me agreeing to follow specific instructions." Nick looked around the den he'd been in maybe one hundred times in the Meg-Nick years—the social events at the Willis apartment, the informal editor/boss meetings.

"I can't believe this happened. And I hate to disappoint Lizzie, but her matchmaking plans might have to be scrapped. Considering I flattened my Liz-intended." Nick forced himself to remove the sarcastic tone from his voice. "Admit it, my decking Reynolds and putting her in the ER is not the best segue into true love. Hell, I bet she never talks to me again."

Jake approached and handed him a bottled water from the bar fridge. "You might think about *not* calling her Reynolds."

"Oh, that. She hasn't objected yet."

Jake didn't respond to the comment. Instead, he sipped his bourbon and looked out the window toward thousands of city lights. Nick wondered how often Jake's gaze settled on the skyline where the Trade Towers had stood. It had been a trying two hours, and he couldn't help but ask, "You ever really get over losing Sam that way, Jake?"

Jake took another sip and turned. "No. Not *over* it. But the pain dulls, the loss settles in a way that allows you to move on, and if you're lucky? If you're lucky, you meet a Lizzie. As far as losing Meg goes"—he paused and leveled his gaze so that Nick felt pinned—"you'll find your way through that on your own. In fact, it seems to me that you're beginning to come out of the darkest part of losing Meg."

"I guess I am. It's weird, though, how you notice it, or even more, *not* noticing it. Like, walking into a room without a sideshow of Meg sitting and reading, or Emily on Meg's lap, the two of them laughing." Nick bit his tongue to keep from asking for a drink after all. Jake continued to stare. "What? Is there something more I should expect in the grieving process?"

"No, it's just that I was thinking."

"And?"

"It's like I said: if you're lucky, you meet someone like Liz. But it could also be the other way around. Like Liz's plan, and if you're Maggie, she meets a Nick Cooper."

"Huh? What are you getting at?"

"Only that I think you should take some time and get to know that neighbor of yours, Coop. She's been through a lot, and so have you. Maybe it sounds trite, but I guess Lizzie's idea is that you can come out of the fire together."

"God, I wish I could have that drink." Nick put his hands in his pockets, hoping the action would stave off the desire to take Jake up on the offer of a shot of whiskey. Hell, he felt like a pint wouldn't settle his nerves, and emotion was already churning the acid in his gut; abstinence remained the better choice. "I can't. And I should get back."

"I agree." Setting his drink glass on a coaster next to a lived-in leather chair, Jake came toward him, and they walked up the two steps to the entryway and the front door.

"Damn, what am I thinking? I need to say goodnight to Em," Nick said.

In sync with his comment, Liz came down the hallway. "Oh, glad I caught you. Emily's fine. We talked about what happened. I didn't sense any problem trauma-wise. She's an amazing kid."

Nick grinned in response to her assessment. "That she is. I should run back and say goodnight."

"Oh, I think it's better you don't."

"Is she that angry at me for clobbering the babysitter?"

"Oh, no. It's not that, but Annie and I got her teeth and hair brushed, her faced washed, and heard the entire story of you trying to kill…"

"Hey, that's a bit over the top."

"Of course it is. That being the case, you're in for a lot of years of high drama. Anyway, we got her tucked in, and I could have sworn she was asleep." Liz paused, and he got the feeling she was drawing the story out just enough to torture him. "But she popped back up. Just like that, adding one last thing."

Jake intervened. "Lizzie, Coop needs to head back to the hospital."

"Oh, right. Sorry. Then quickly? She thinks you should marry Maggie."

Nick could tell Liz was about to burst out laughing. He didn't anticipate an I-told-you-so from Jake but did turn and catch a quick but smug look on Jake's face.

"You two are seriously annoying as friends sometimes, you know that?"

Jake and Liz responded in tandem, "Yep." And then Jake pulled open the door to the interior hallway of the building. "Hold on, Coop. Don't worry about all of our teasing. Just make sure Maggie's okay, and let us know when she's settled and you're free so we can bring Emily back."

"I will."

Nick walked toward the elevator, with a final wave to their goodbyes and good lucks as the lift doors whispered shut. After he hit the big "G" for Garage, he had a chance to close his eyes. With his back resting against the elevator wall, he wondered at the image that appeared in his head. Reynolds. Maybe Jake was right about using the surname thing, especially when an image of Maggie in those goofy exercise shorts and a t-shirt, sitting at the edge of her kitchen counter, popped into his head. He could still see the gash cutting into the soft skin of her thigh. He'd wanted to kiss her then, and now that he'd kissed her once, he knew he wanted more.

He spoke to the empty elevator. "I'm tired." He must be. How else could anyone explain the fact of his thinking of actually asking the woman out on a date? "Damn it." It was the treachery of human nature, and as an editor of fiction, he should know better. All the trite phrases he ex'd out of books; the comments he made in margins about tamping down flowery prose. And now, despite years of derisive thinking of the happily-ever-after romance, his heart was pounding like any hero's would from the pages of a book. He exited the elevator, taking deep breaths as he trotted to his car. "Dial it back, Nick," he muttered to himself.

"Sir?" A security man stood there, looking at him warily.

"Oh, sorry, you caught me talking to myself." Nick continued toward his SUV, which he considered a necessity rather than a luxury. Its sleek Jaguar emblem on the back, the lean lines, and deep blue paint job didn't exactly scream "The Dad Car." But Em loved it because they got to drive in a "big cat."

"You have a visitor sticker?" Mr. Security asked.

"On the front dash. I was seeing Jake Willis."

"Great. Thanks for the information. You be safe now."

"Appreciate it." Nick hit the key fob, and the familiar beep of his door locks opening allowed his escape from the vigilant but over-friendly building security man. As he settled into the seat, he waved and closed the door.

Nick realized he was safe, he had good friends, and he was starting to enjoy living. Whatever her secrets were, and the past hinted at by Jake a few moments ago, Nick was going to figure out if Ms. Maggie Reynolds wanted to do the same thing.

CHAPTER SIXTEEN

Home from the ER

Maggie watched blearily as the safety belt was clicked around her waist. Mmm, this man smelled *good*. Not musky and scary, not stale and sweaty, just good. It was unusual for Ricky.

She blinked. Hell no, she wasn't with Ricky. Ricky was dead and gone.

"You warm enough?"

The question was murmured with Coop leaning so close to her face she could see the shadowy outline of a five o'clock beard. His jaw was taut with concern. Barely able to keep her eyes open, Maggie gulped as he reached over from the open passenger door, between the two front seats, and pulled a coat out from behind. His left shoulder pressed into hers to complete the motion, and it felt like she was flying down a zip line.

"Let's make sure anyway." He tucked the long wool coat around her body with large hands, first at her hips and thighs. With her eyes closed, she dreamily visualized Coop without a shirt on. The vision was so real she moved her hands as if to touch him, but the coat was in the way.

"Easy, Reynolds. You're going to have to be still. And I have to figure out how we can take care of you for a few days."

Maybe she replied; Maggie wasn't sure. But if she had spoken, it must have been funny because he chuckled.

Her head became a little less fuzzy when her stomach kicked in. "I think I'm hungry."

"You might be. I don't know what all you and Emily ate at the apartment before I threw my punch, but you've been in the ER for a couple of hours. I imagine that's long enough to have worked up an appetite."

"You look funny."

"No. You can only see out of one eye right now. The doctors put on an eye patch. They said I can take it off for you when we get back to my apartment. It's because the hospital lights are so bright."

"No. You just don't look like you."

Images, the last things she remembered, tugged at the edges of her mind. Opening the door with Emily. "Emily?"

"She's fine. Tucked in at Jake and Lizzie's house." He tugged on the shoulder strap of her seat belt; it locked. "Okay, that's working. Now, let's get you home."

"Why would I go home with you? I don't ev..." His finger shushed her against her mouth. The touch sent a warm sensation flowing from her forehead to her toes. What was that saying at the end of the wizard movie, the one with flying monkeys? There was an Emily in that, and a little dog. No, it was a Dorothy. There was a man without a heart. Like Ricky. This man wasn't Ricky; he was too kind. And there'd been a witch. "Melting, I'm melting."

"No, you're just tired and hungry." He folded himself out of her side of the car, then leaned back in for a second. "You just relax. You'll be in those koala slippers before you know it."

How does he know about my slippers? Her mind grappled with a memory. Nick-Coop at her door; she was wearing the slippers then. *Right.*

The car door opened on the driver's side, and Maggie realized she must have dozed off for however long it took him to walk around the car and get in because there he was. She turned her head a little to watch him, but it hurt. The car pinged its "door open" noise while he settled in. She heard the seatbelt click, then the door slammed shut. The key turned, and she heard the blinker, which meant they must have pulled away from wherever they were.

"I don't remember dinner. Did I spoil it?"

"No. We didn't go out to eat, Maggie."

"Oh, was it something I said?" She heard herself giggle.

"You've been at the hospital, in the ER. You have a mild concussion, some stitches in the back of your head, and a bruise around your right eye. They gave you something for pain."

"Shit."

She heard him release a long, slow breath. "Yeah, that's one way to put it."

Maggie shifted her weight in the seat, thankful that, for whatever reason, she was being driven away from the hospital. She wracked her brain, even though it hurt, to figure out what started it this time. The fight. Ricky getting all pissed off. She was in pain, so she must have done something stupid. Otherwise, Ricky wouldn't have hit her. Well, usually it was something she did. Okay, that wasn't always true. Sometimes—sometimes, there wasn't a reason.

She shook her head, hating herself for being stupid and trying to stop the flood of rumination that haunted her after Ricky went off.

Maggie tried focusing on something else, keeping her eyes squeezed shut as if that made her invisible. She noticed she was warm. *The seat is heated. We got a new car?*

Well, she wouldn't bring it up. She should—they didn't need a new car. Just like Ricky to do that. Make a major decision without her, knowing that his loving wife was *Ms. Mousey Maggie.* She wouldn't mention it to him, wouldn't put up a fight about it.

And the hospital again? *Wasn't I just there two weeks ago?*

A tear slid down her cheek. God, she hated the ER. The cluck-clucks and the lectures. Everyone always wanted to help her, get her out of the place that caused her injury and pain. Everyone. But they'd never tried it themselves. Never packed a suitcase and then had to shove it under the bed because they'd heard Ricky's key in the lock. She was trapped. So many business cards and folded notes had been tucked into her hand, with whispers like, "Here's my number, call me," or, "This is my brother's number. He's a police officer. Please, call him." Always nice, except it also felt condescending. *Dammit. I won't cry. I won't. I won't.* But she could feel the moisture on her cheeks.

He must have smacked her good this time because her head was pounding, and she couldn't see out of one eye.

The car rolled to a stop, and she felt the subtle shift from drive to park. A warm hand covered the clenched fist she was pounding rhythmically against her thigh.

"Hey, hey, what is it? What's wrong, Reynolds?"

He was using her maiden name, so he must be über-angry with her. God, she didn't want him to beat her again, not tonight anyway. She just needed to rest, to heal up a little. So, she did what she always did, said what she always said. "Ricky? Whatever I did, I'm sorry. I'm so sorry…"

***

She was sleeping on his sofa, bundled into a soft, warm blanket. The doc had said she could sleep as long as someone watched over her for the first few hours. It gave Nick a chance to re-think all that had happened in five hours. Not from the punch, but from the point of getting Maggie into the ER and the weird things since then.

Like, who the hell was Ricky, and why was he worthy of such an apology? Okay, he must be the Amato in Maggie's past, the name on the letter? Except that had been "T. Amato." More importantly, why did Maggie have prior visit records at the hospital?

He retraced events, like when he'd waited for Maggie to be taken care of at the ER, sitting with her, trying to figure out how he was going to get forgiveness for smacking her in the eye.

Then there'd been that one nurse. The RN who'd kept eyeing him like he was an ogre. She'd done the same thing before he left to take Emily to Jake and Liz's.

Then, when he'd had Maggie in the wheelchair, ready to roll her down to his car, another nurse took him aside. "I swear, sir, if she comes back here again, and you're with her? I'm calling the police."

Before he could protest, an orderly had come in with all the necessary discharge papers, and the threatening RN disappeared.

Slugging through the discharge papers now, the shot of bourbon he'd previously rejected at Jake's sat next to his right arm, ice cubes melting because of his getting engrossed with the details of aftercare.

It turned out retrospect was easier to manage than when things were happening rapid-fire at the hospital. Like when they'd arrived at the ER. He'd been standing behind Maggie's chair when they took the basics—her insurance card, personal information, name, address, DOB.

She'd remained calm through the intake process until they looked her up by date of birth and noted prior visits under a different name. Her response had been visceral. "I'm not Maggie Amato. I'm Maggie Reynolds. I haven't used Amato in years."

The administrator's response, a bit snooty as far as Nick was concerned, had at least been straightforward. "Then who do we put as your emergency contact?"

It was funny. Okay, not that funny. She had pointed behind her and said, "Him. We live together. Nicholas Cooper. Coop. Same address."

Nick's new cover was at least useful, and he'd been able to provide his phone number and, with the fake relationship, have access to some information. He'd had to marshal all his patience about the Amato thing. *Maggie was definitely married before. A strange thing not to mention.*

His curiosity had been rapid-firing questions in his brain, but then they'd put her in a wheelchair and were rolling her away. He'd tapped the chair's driver on the shoulder. "Excuse me?"

The attendant had turned and stared at him inhospitably, which made no sense, but at the time, Nick hadn't cared. "I'm sorry," Nick had said. "We're here with my daughter. I'd like to take her to a friend's and come back. Is that going to be okay?"

Mr. Wheelchair-Pusher had responded curtly, "Yes." He'd looked at the clipboard pressed into Maggie's lap. "It's fine. They'll be doing X-rays, maybe even scans, so she'll be here awhile. Check in at the front desk when you come back." That was it. He'd rolled Maggie off, and Nick hadn't had much chance to think about it since then.

He should have taken the opportunity when he dropped Emily off with Liz and Jake to ask about the Amato name and a prior marriage, but then Jake had clammed up and said that Nick needed to ask Maggie about her past.

The fall backwards had done the greater damage, and he was relieved she'd be ok after hitting her head like that on his tiled entrance.

He ran both hands through his hair, glad the worst seemed over. After slugging his drink, he set the glass down and walked over to the woman sleeping on his sofa.

At five-eleven, her form took up two-thirds of the big sectional. And thin. But not skinny. She had curves, her neck was long, and her collar bones, showing a bit above the blanket's edge and the rounded neckline of her shirt, were sexy as hell.

Damn.

Maggie Reynolds—from top to bottom—was one beautiful woman.

***

"Hey, Coop." Maggie sat up and tossed the blanket that covered her onto the end of the sofa. She stretched her arms over her head, watching him as he came out of the bathroom. *My bathroom?* No, she was at Coop's. Her head hurt, and the memories of the ER visit started filling in the blanks.

"You're awake," Coop said. "Good. I bet you're hungry."

"Stupid people aren't allowed to eat," she snapped.

"Oh, we can make exceptions."

"I don't know why."

"How 'bout because I'm the one that knocked you out and landed you on the floor."

"Oh. Right. I guess there's that."

He grinned at her, and Maggie felt fuzzy and warm. She realized he couldn't have done much to take care of his needs since…when? "What time is it?"

Coop glanced at his watch. "Eight thirty."

"What day?"

"The next one." He laughed. The kind of laughter that made a person feel like everything was going to be all right.

But it wasn't all right. Teddy Amato was still out there. He knew where she lived. He hated her and wanted her dead. The recollection of her hospital visit brought it all back. Teddy filling Ricky's shoes.

But that wasn't the worst of it. Nope. The really bad part? Maggie was falling in love with her neighbor. He had a beautiful daughter. Neither of them should be involved in the mess she'd made of her life. "So, it's Saturday, then?"

"Yep."

She leaned back, closing her eyes, and must have spaced out because the next thing she knew, Coop was putting a plate in front of her on the coffee table.

"God, is that sugar on top?"

"Total sugar. Bad sugar. It's toast dosed with cinnamon sugar. It always works to cure what ails me."

"No way. You have some kind of secret sugar thing?"

"No secret, Reynolds. I love coffee cake the most. But don't leave me alone with a bag of oatmeal cookies or a molten lava cake either."

"So, you're not prejudiced against the form of your sugar?"

"Nope. I even love those little Frosted Mini-Wheat things."

Maggie relaxed. Neither of them had approached the proverbial elephant in the room, let alone conquered it. And Maggie knew now she couldn't keep Coop in the dark about her past. If nothing else, she had to tell him so that Teddy Amato didn't come after Emily.

It meant she couldn't fall in love with Coop.

It meant she had to tell him everything.

It meant she had to move away.

CHAPTER SEVENTEEN

Admissions

Reluctantly, Coop had let Maggie go back to her apartment to shower and change. He'd made her promise she wouldn't wash her hair because of the stitches, despite the fact it was matted in the back. Just for twenty-four hours.

She now stood in the doorway to her bedroom. He was sitting on her sofa, reading a paper draft of some manuscript. Maggie had to admit the shower had felt better just knowing he was in the apartment, but it didn't ease her conundrum.

The eye patch had been temporary, and she was happy it had peeled off without too much sticky tape residue. Now, with the finishing touches on her face, tinted sunscreen, a hint of soft brown eyeshadow, button-down cotton shirt loose over fresh jeans, and her hair back in a pony tail, she headed toward the living room area.

"Hi."

Coop looked up, then stood, putting his copy of the book on the coffee table. "Ah, you look better. Were you careful washing your face?"

"I followed the directions, Dr. Cooper." She flashed him a smile. "I didn't wash my hair, just let it get damp from the steam, so just ignore what's behind the scrunchie." She reached up to make sure her matt of hair was secure. "Ow. Damn this lump on my head. What a comedy."

"It is kind of funny in retrospect"—he looked down at his shoes—"but, again, I'm sorry."

"Enough, Coop. It was an accident." She slid into a chair at her dining room table, not noticing he'd come up behind her until the subtle woodsy aroma that was his signature aftershave hit her senses.

His hands began to gently rub the tops of both of her shoulders. When his fingers moved to dig lightly under her shoulder blades, she couldn't stop the deep sigh that escaped her mouth.

"It's okay," he said. "The ER folks said you'd be sore, not just from the bump on your head but from landing shoulders-first on the floor."

"I did that?"

"Yes, and I'm sorry, Maggie."

"Have I told you a bunch of times yet not to be?"

"A handful."

"So, Editor-man, you're a little slow on picking up on things?"

But he wasn't. Coop turned the chair and pulled Maggie to her feet. With her height, they were nearly eye to eye. She only had to tilt her head a little to be trapped by the look in his eyes. Maggie couldn't have moved if her feet were on fire.

The tension that had been like opposing magnetic poles between them melted away. She let her body lean into his even as he gently pulled her pony tail back for the kiss. And it was a kiss. Tender, soft, a little nibble on her lower lip, his mouth moved to her nose and touched it lightly before settling back on her lips. Maggie's pulse raced, and the sensation from his mouth against hers sent a rush of heat all the way to her toes.

Coop pulled back. He looked at her for reassurance, and all she could say was, "It's okay, Coop. It's okay."

His fingers found the buttons of her blouse, and purposefully, but without rushing, he undid each one, down to her jeans. Coop's right index finger traced her skin from one bra strap across to the other, following the outline of her bra, and then he cupped each breast as if she were fragile.

"I won't break, you know," she said.

"Oh, but you might. I mean, I smashed your face, and you wound up on the floor. It's my fault you cracked your head open."

She raised a hand to his face, felt the stubble there, and realized he hadn't shaved. "I guess I disrupted your routine. You and Emily seem to have a perfect schedule, you're so close."

"We had a schedule to survive losing Meg."

She wondered at his matter-of-fact delivery regarding the loss of his wife.

His voice grew husky. "We've been putting one foot down in front of another for too long. It's about time I switch things up a little."

"Is this…" Maggie swept her hands from her shoulders down to her waist. "…switching things up a little?" She didn't mean to sound short, but hearing her own tone, she couldn't help but jump to an apology. "Dammit, I'm sorry. That sounded terrible. You didn't deserve that."

He grabbed her hands and pulled them up in his to hold them against his chest. "I need to know about you, everything. Jake filled me in only on the fact that you've had a bad time. And from your ER records, you've been there before. Somebody hurt you. Bad. But not now. I'm not interrupting this for anything."

She understood how he felt. Maggie didn't want her past or future to tame the heat she was feeling. The need. Maybe it was the last few weeks and all the weird, scary shit from Ricky's brother. Maybe it was being back in an ER last night, a place she'd never thought she'd have to go again. Whatever it was, Maggie wasn't going to let it interfere with his touches.

"Coop?"

His stare was intense. "Yes?"

"At this moment, now, I don't think I've ever wanted anything more in my life"—she took a deep breath—"than you."

"You're one hundred percent sure? Not ninety-nine, not ninety-eight—" He was counting down, each time placing a light kiss on her face, his fingers resting gently against her neck. "Ninety-three…"

"I'm sure. One hundred perc…"

His strength surprised Maggie—that he could pick her up and carry her into the bedroom boggled her mind.

Coop set her down to stand by the bed while he removed his shirt. She had to bite her lip to prevent the gasp that would otherwise have escaped from seeing him shirtless.

The silly phrase from some movie stuck in her head: "You work out?" Cripes, did he ever. He had a broad chest and shoulders, and there was no fat she could see. Not anywhere.

He caught her staring and grinned. "Okay for an old man?"

She was sure she turned three shades of red from the hot flush she felt. He didn't take his eyes off her as he undid the top button on his jeans. Sometime in this process, he'd kicked off his shoes. Coop pulled her closer by tugging on her beltloops.

She couldn't help herself. "How old?"

"Are you worried about our age difference?"

"No. I only have to think of Lizzie and Jake not to be. I'm just curious because"—she paused—"because you're…uh, well…"

Pausing, he kissed her forehead, her nose, the space between her breasts at the sternum. Still, he didn't slip her bra off despite the obvious expression of desire that her taut nipples revealed against the fabric. "You like what you see, Reynolds? I know I want to see more of you." His voice was husky against her skin. "I'm forty-four. That okay?" His mouth covered a nipple through the fabric.

"Sweet mercy, Coop." She reached for him, hoping to pull him against her, but his hands grabbed her wrists as he moved his mouth back up her neck. His tongue flicked into one of her ears, and this time, she didn't care what sound came out of her mouth. She was losing strength in her knees.

He scooped her up again and laid her on the bed. "If you hurt anywhere, you have to tell me." She shook her head from side to side: a no. After unbuttoning her jeans, he pulled off the ridiculous koala bear slippers, which might have spoiled the mood but for the wicked grin that preceded his tossing one each to opposite corners of the room. Maggie stared, entranced as he slid his jeans off his hips and, holding them in one hand, pulled out a strip-package of condoms, making her wonder how long he'd been planning this seduction.

Except she didn't give a damn. She wriggled out of her jeans and then lay still.

Coop knelt on either side of her, his stare a tractor beam she couldn't escape. She reached to grab at her underwear, but he slipped them off and found her most sensitive spot with two fingers, and in only a couple of minutes, she was consumed with unbearable heat. She moaned loudly at the welcome sensation, and before she knew it, he was in her, thrusting fiercely, then groaning in her ear. "Oh. My. God. Maggie."

He collapsed on top of her, and she wrapped her arms around him as if he were a lifeline. A tear ran down one of her cheeks. Somehow the connection between them meant more to her *because* he'd lost all control. A fleeting thought that anytime it had ever happened to Ricky, he'd jumped off of her, screaming that it was her effing fault. Most times, he'd called her a stupid bitch, and sometimes he'd smacked her for it.

She marveled at the fact that Coop had not been able to stop himself and the fact it was her who had ignited his passion so completely.

Neither of them moved for two or three minutes. His breathing slowed, and he whispered in her ear, his breath warm, "God, Maggie. That's…" He took a deep breath. "Never happened to me before."

Her fingers moved in a circular motion across the skin of his left shoulder. Likewise, her brain ran ideas through her head of what to say. She didn't care about the lovemaking, only that they were together. The longing she had for Coop wasn't centered on sex. She was in awe of the intimacy she felt with him in her arms—she'd never had that before.

He propped himself up on his elbows and stared at her with an intensity that pinned her to the pillow. "I haven't been with anyone since Meg."

His sheepish embarrassment, the sincerity—the fact he'd chosen her after losing this person he'd loved so deeply—humbled her, and she reached up and touched his face. "I'm honored, Coop."

He stirred against her, his body changing from soft to hard, his desire sending blood rushing through him again.

"And it's okay. I'm not going anywhere." And she didn't.

***

The room was dark, and she realized that at some point, Coop must have pulled the covers up over her to let her sleep. They'd made love again, slower this time, and sated, they'd lain next to each other and talked until she must have drifted off.

The unveiling of their hurts, the emotion that tagged along behind each revelation shared—with a gentleness Maggie had never known existed, Coop had touched the places where Ricky had beaten her. And she had reciprocated by quietly listening as he described the last month of Meg's life, the pain he could only witness but never take away from the woman he loved. Coop had talked about how he and Meg met, and it didn't hurt when he mentioned how deeply he'd loved his wife.

In turn, he'd cajoled the past from Maggie, the truth about Ricky Amato and her years of hell. Again, he'd gently caress places where she had scars, including the long line from belly button to right hip where Ricky had thought she'd learn something if he ran a knife point along her skin.

Maggie hadn't told Coop about Teddy, though. She hadn't wanted to spoil how much they were learning about each other between cat naps and making love. It wasn't an omission; there just wasn't time.

She remembered getting up to go to the bathroom when Coop went to the kitchen and brought them glasses of juice.

"That's cheating, Mags," he'd said, commenting on the fact that she'd rinsed her mouth and put on a t-shirt and running shorts in his absence.

"I'm still shy in your presence, Coop."

"At least I'm assured you're not a clothes horse."

She'd been ready to toss a pillow at him for the remark but remembered the two glasses of juice. He'd handed her one, and she'd been swallowing when he added, "And I think with practice, practice, practice, we can have you so comfortable around me that you'll lounge about naked and eat bonbons on your days off." His grin was so suggestive she'd sneezed orange juice through her nose in a fit of giggles. She'd run to the shower, and he'd followed.

Maggie remembered soap everywhere and his hands roving over her skin, his body pressed against hers in the heat and steam of the pounding spray. He'd been careful to turn her head away from the stream of water as his fingers took a path to her most vulnerable spot, bringing her to an explosion of sensation so that her knees went weak, and he'd had to hold her up until the spasms ceased.

He'd dried her then, and when she reached for a nightie from somewhere in her top drawer, he'd stopped her. "T-shirt and running shorts, please."

Coop had also had the good grace not to laugh at her when she'd insisted on straightening up the bed before they climbed back in. He'd wrapped his arms around her, snuggling, his stomach against her back. It hadn't felt weird to her when he said, "Do you like children, Reynolds?"

"Of course I do. I'm a grade school teacher, for crying out loud."

"Oh, that's not a guarantee. I had several ogres in my early years."

"Maybe you were a precocious and obnoxious child."

The rumbling laugh that had vibrated against her back made Maggie believe she could feel safe in a man's arms.

"I was only asking because I come with a seven-year-old with a skill set resembling the Spanish Inquisition."

Maggie remembered laughing, answering, "I love Emily."

Maybe her admission was the commitment he'd been looking for because he'd pulled her close and confessed, "Good. Because I think I'm falling in love with you. I thought you should know that."

She remembered perfectly how she had turned and found his face in the darkness. "Can I call you Nick sometimes?"

"Sure. I guess it's a bit like the reverse of Reynolds."

"Good, because Nicholas, Nick, Coop, Cooper? I think I'm falling for you too."

***

It must have been after one when they finally slept. And maybe that was why her head felt odd. She fought to come out of a brain fog so that she could talk to Coop more, hold him…

Her mouth tasted funny. She wasn't sure why. Had Coop given her some of the pain medication after all? She didn't think so. They'd covered the pain later when lying in bed. "How's your head? Does this hurt?" She recalled Coop's careful examination. It had made her smile. For some reason, any pain had melted away at his touch.

But now, her head pounded, her neck was sore, and her wrists were throbbing.

Maggie yawned, and a jolt of pain stabbed on the left side of her face. Her jaw felt sore. Not where Coop had accidentally smacked her in the right eye. No, this was pain on the other side.

Had Coop left to go get Emily?

No, they were up too late.

Noises drifted in but sounded far off. The door to her bedroom must be closed. She heard a pan clang, water ran, and the sounds made her hungry—famished in fact. Coop must be making them something to eat. She still felt groggy but told herself to get up, quietly. Even change into something besides jogging shorts and the ratty t-shirt. No, her silly outfit turned Coop on. She needed to get up so she could surprise Coop in the kitchen.

No, that couldn't be right. They got up together, she remembered it. Coop cracking eggs. She was going to make toast. Teddy Amato in her kitchen.

What the hell had Teddy Amato been doing in her kitchen?

Oh. My. God. Fear spiked, her stomach roiling with it. Maggie tried turning, thinking of putting her feet on the ground.

But she was stuck. Her hands were zip-tied to a bed. She felt the frame: metal. She remembered it and knew the room. She and Ricky had slept here once or twice. The house near the river.

Irrational as it was, terror struck, real and chilling—she couldn't stop it.

Teddy.

The door to the bedroom slammed open all the way, revealing a tall, lean figure silhouetted by the light behind him. "Hey, Mags. You're up."

She couldn't breathe.

"You know, you're still a bitch after all this time?" Teddy said. "Imagine my surprise when I found you with neighbor boy in your kitchen. Well, technically, he'd just stepped into the living room when I knocked his fucking block off. And worse: you put those beautiful roses I delivered in the closet? Like I said, total bitch."

"What have you done to Coop?"

"Cutesy nickname? Whatever. But he'll live. Just a little tap to the back of his head with the butt of my piece."

"Where am I, Teddy?"

"Ya know, Maggie, I could tell you that, but it won't do you any good. And lover boy will never find you. In fact, when I'm through with you, Mags? There'll be nothing to find." Teddy grinned, threw what appeared to be loose clothes on the floor, then turned. He hit the light switch and slammed the door behind him.

Once again alone in the dark, Maggie wondered what the hell she was supposed to do with a bunch of stupid clothes.

She tugged at the zip ties again, swallowing bile and trying to fight the terror she felt inside. She needed to escape, somehow, because there was no doubt in her mind that Ricky's crazy brother, Teddy, intended to kill her.

CHAPTER EIGHTEEN

Out of Control

Nick woke up with a headache. On the floor. Something was wrong. Grabbing the end of the sofa, he got up slowly, surveying his surroundings. Dim light filtered in through a window. It must be after dawn, although a light was still on over the stove.

Not my apartment. That he wasn't home sent a "be wary" warning down his spine. He was in Reynolds's place. Jeans, but no shirt. *What the hell?*

"Reynolds, you here?" Silence.

"Maggie?" Memories came back to him. *We made love. More than once.* He wasn't shocked at the recollection. In fact, it struck him with a sense of awe. Nick hadn't just *made* love to Maggie. He was *in love* with her; the acceptance of this realization made the current situation more challenging.

He found and flipped up the light switch for the living room and dining area, bringing the empty apartment back into focus. After their hours of lovemaking, sleeping, and more of the same, they'd gotten out of bed to make something to eat.

A recollection of Maggie in those goofy running shorts and a tank top, bending into the fridge, brought a quick flush of desire. That image was instantly wiped away by the picture in his head of some guy standing by the table, pointing a gun at Nick. Maggie, in shock, all she offered was a weak, "Teddy."

Nick remembered rushing him, head down, like his football days of twenty-plus years earlier. He made contact with the asshole at about waist level but was surprised at the sinewy strength of the creep. Surprised until everything went black. He raised his left hand to the back of his head, and there it was—a big fat lump.

Knowing it was pointless, he still raced through the apartment, checking Maggie's bedroom and the bathroom. Nothing. Nick stood next to the dining room table, scared and frustrated, his mind racing with the possibilities.

"The closet." He hadn't checked the entry closet. It was stupid; she wouldn't be there, but he threw it open anyway.

He noted an empty hanger in between two other long coats. Teddy must have covered her with a coat. Shaking his head, he looked down.

"What the hell?" He punched the wall in frustration. On the floor of the closet was a vase of dying roses. He reached for a card sticking up from the arrangement but pulled his hand back as if burned. Any hope of finding Maggie would be tied up in forensic evidence. He knew that much.

The time period from his waking up dazed and his standing now at her front door was maybe five minutes. He had to act, not touch anything, and call the cops.

Nick ran back to the bedroom and found his cell phone. Seeing the still-rumpled bed made his heart ache. Mags was gone, and somebody named Teddy had her. Again he wondered, was Teddy the one who'd sent the letters? T. Amato?

He dialed 911 and relayed the facts as best he knew them, and that Maggie had been kidnapped.

And then he called Jake Willis.

CHAPTER NINETEEN

Maggie's Gone

"Caldwell here."

Jake sighed in relief at hearing his friend's voice. Detective Trevor Caldwell and his wife were one of Liz's famous Christmas matches. Moreover, despite that connection, and being a good friend, Jake knew Trevor had the credentials to understand the situation he was in.

"Hey, Trevor. It's Jake Willis."

"Been awhile, Jake, but I recognized your voice."

"It's good to know you're still on your toes, especially now that you have kids and some grey hair."

"Says who?"

"Your wife, Trev. At least according to Lizzie."

"Well, she'd know. Angie said she had lunch with Liz a couple of weeks ago. Made me think we were due for a beer."

"Yes. Listen, Trev. I'd love to catch up, but we've got a situation."

"What's up?"

"You might even already be on board. I'm told it's been assigned to two of your detectives." Jake took a breath. "I was hoping you could keep your eye on it since it involves a mutual friend." He hadn't been sure how receptive Trevor would be to an outsider's request, but he had no choice. It was Maggie. "It's important."

"So, do you know the names of the detectives who caught the case?"

"No—" Jake didn't, but he continued, "I know NYPD did that major restructuring in 2016, and it should qualify for your Major Case Squad. Aren't you still a hostage negotiator…?"

"Among other things. Robbery gone south?"

"No. Kidnapping. Well, he took her against her will, anyway. The asshole has also threatened to kill her in the past." Trevor didn't say anything, and Jake figured he was running through some scenarios in his head, so he added, "I'm pretty sure you know the girl that's missing."

"You want to cut to the chase here, Jake?"

There was no point in making Trevor drag information from him, so he spit it out. "It's Maggie Reynolds."

Silence, unless he counted the expletive, a squeak from Trevor's chair, and then the feverish tapping into a keyboard. "Crap. I thought that scumbag husband of hers died in prison."

More typing.

"He did." Liz had come into the den, and although Jake didn't really want her to hear one half of the conversation, he signaled his wife to sit. He would catch hell for not filling her in before he called Trevor, but time was critical, and all of NYPD's resources needed to hit the ground running. Liz would just have to forgive him for calling Trevor as soon as he'd hung up with Coop. "You remember the brother? Teddy Amato? I'd be surprised if he doesn't have a record. Liz told me just the other day he's been making threats regarding Maggie. My guess? He's the one who grabbed her."

Liz leaped up from the loveseat across the room from Jake's desk. She was turning red, and Jake cupped his hand over the phone. "Hang on, Lizzie, and I'll explain."

"Jake?" Trevor's gruff voice echoed on the phone.

"Yes, I'm here."

"Can you hold on while I make a few calls? I want to get things rolling."

"Yeah, sure. That'll give me a few minutes to talk with Liz." Trevor was gone, and now all Jake heard was canned music.

Liz was pacing, wearing a hole in the carpet of his office. "And just when were you going to tell me, Jake Willis?"

"As soon as I could. I got the call from Coop, hung up, and called Trevor. You can understand why I had to do things in that order."

She stopped her in-circles trek. "Yeah, okay. I get it. But hearing it like that, out of nowhere, it's freaking me out."

"Of course it is. But you know Trev is a great detective."

Liz again plopped down on the overstuffed loveseat. She was anchored between the sofa's arms and two end tables with reading lamps. The wall of books that represented Jake's bread and butter ran in shelves from floor to ceiling on either side of the end tables. A painting of Chincoteague Island hung behind Liz as she curled her feet onto the sofa, then grabbed a throw pillow and punched it with all her might. "Has Trev told Angie? I mean, she and Maggie still teach at the same school." She barely took a breath. "And Maggie must be terrified. You don't think she's dead, do you? Oh, God."

He would have joined her, held her, but he was listening to canned music and waiting for Trevor to come back on the line.

"You know," Liz continued, "when Coop called last night and asked us to keep Emily another day or two, I just had the best feeling ever. Like for sure he and Maggie had connected."

"Well, I don't know all the details," Jake said, "but I do know that Coop was in Maggie's apartment when he got knocked cold."

"What?" She jumped up again. "You didn't tell me. Is Coop okay?"

"Lizzie, when exactly could I?" While Jake understood her anxiety, she had to wait. He held up his hand to halt their conversation. "Trev? Yeah."

"Jake?" Not waiting for confirmation, Trevor added, "I've now confirmed who's assigned to the case, and it will stay with Major Crimes."

"Good, that's good, Trev. Is anything new?"

"Yes. We got info back on Amato, and he's got some juvenile charges, all misdemeanors, kid stuff, tipping over trash cans, truancy, but nothing that hints at kidnapping."

"Yes, but…"

"I don't mean to be rude, but let me get the details out first, Jake."

"Sorry, go on," Jake said.

Liz sat on the edge of the sofa. Her fear for Maggie was evident. She was chewing on a fingernail.

"The good news is Teddy did some time," Trevor said. "Burglary—his was charged as third-degree, so he could have been sentenced for up to seven years. He wasn't. He was drunk, his brother had been killed in prison, he expressed remorse, nobody was hurt, he didn't take anything…"

"I'm sorry, Trev. He didn't take anything?"

"I know it confuses people, but all you need for a burglary charge in this state is the *intent* to commit a crime in someone else's house or place of business."

"Okay. But isn't it still a felony?"

"Yeah, but he hadn't been charged with anything since he was sixteen, and the judge only gave Teddy a year."

"Shit." Jake immediately wished he hadn't sworn. It perked Liz up like a lioness protecting her cubs. He mouthed, "Hold on, babe," and refocused on Trevor's voice.

"I know that's frustrating, Jake, but it is good news to some extent."

Impressed with Trevor's patience, Jake only offered, "How so?"

"Well, although he didn't serve the whole year, he had a parole officer for a while."

"So, you have addresses, hang-outs, possibly contacts with family or friends."

"One address anyway. But it gives us a place to start. It's the same house he and Ricky grew up in. Looks like dear old mommy died and left it to her boys." Trevor cleared his throat, making Jake think bad news was next. "I don't like folks to get their hopes up too high, though. It could be a dead end with the time that's passed. And Teddy has no friends. No family. All of which concerns me because he has no filters, no one to talk to, and he spent eight months in prison with nothing to do but stew about Ms. Reynolds."

Jake didn't speak. He didn't dare give these details to Liz. The worry in Caldwell's voice spoke volumes. Maggie was in real danger.

"Bottom line? We're working on some leads, Jake. Take down my mobile number because I'm going to be out beating bushes for intel."

Jotting the digits down on his note pad, Jake said, "You have my cell, Trev? I'd appreciate updates if and when you get a chance."

"Is that the one ending in 6312?"

"Yeah."

"I got it. And I gotta go."

"Thanks, Trev." The phone on the detective's end had clicked off, leaving Jake to hope Trevor at least heard his thanks.

Jake put the landline receiver back in its cradle, feeling weary. Coop's call had come around dawn, when Jake had been setting the coffee pot to brew and heard his office phone ring. Despite the circumstances, he looked up and smiled at Liz. "At least Trevor and Angie are doing great."

She swiped at a tear. "I know. I just saw Angie." Jake watched as Liz's facial muscles relaxed. "Can you believe they got together— remember we talked about it four years ago? One of my better matches if I do say so myself."

"Yes, it was."

Her worried look returned. "When can we get more information about Maggie?"

"Trust Trevor, sweetheart. He'll do everything he can."

He joined her on the loveseat. Liz leaned against the arm and put her heels in his lap. They were quiet for a few minutes while Jake rubbed her feet. He watched as some of the worry lines on her face eased a little. Thinking to distract her from the Maggie situation, he added, "And so how many people have you invited to this New Year's Eve bash?"

Liz let out a hoot. "Oh, a few."

"Oh, for crying out loud, Liz, from what I gathered, there will hardly be anyone in Times Square."

She had the decency to look chagrined. "Okay, you're right, but it's not going to be like a sit-down dinner at Christmas. That gathering was getting too big, you know that." They sat quietly again, but then the worried look returned to her face. "I'm scared for Maggie."

Liz had put on her brave face, the one that made her look like she was in total control. It might have fooled some people, but she couldn't get away with it where Jake was concerned. "Maybe some good news will help," he said.

"Such as?"

"So far, Trevor's barely scratched the surface investigation-wise, but his preliminary efforts have yielded two things."

Liz sat up straighter. "Tell me."

"According to Teddy Amato's parole officer, Teddy lives in the same house he grew up in. Their mother left it to both boys when she died, and he still lives there."

"What does that have to do with the price of tea in China?"

"Oops, sorry. I forgot you're missing a few steps." She punched him lightly on the thigh, and Jake grabbed her hand, holding it. "The evidence they found in Maggie's apartment." He watched Liz closely. He knew his wife was tough, but she and Maggie were like sisters, and the threatening note, the roses, all of it could tip Liz's feelings from worried to terrified. "Teddy's the one who took Maggie."

"Shit."

Liz tried to free herself from Jake's hold, but he managed to keep her feet in his hands, and she settled again. "Lizzie, you know stomping around the room doesn't help anything." He continued rubbing her left arch, pressing with his thumbs.

Releasing a deep breath, Liz leaned back against the soft cushions of the loveseat. "What a jerk. You know what a complete asshole Teddy is. They have to get him right away." She closed her eyes for a minute, and Jake thought his massage was working.

"It's not even the jerk part of Teddy that worries me," she continued. "He's dangerous. You know he started threatening Maggie right after Ricky's trial, and it escalated when Ricky was murdered in prison. We both thought she was finally safe, but that took her moving three times, going back to her maiden name. Geeze, I thought time would make a difference."

"Not if that grudge of his is deep-set, and certainly not if he's as twisted as it appears."

"Trust me. Teddy is totally fucked up in the head."

He knew that with Liz cursing and using the ultimate "F" word, which she hated, he had little chance of changing the track of her thinking.

"You know he hates her," she said. "Teddy wants Maggie dead."

Jake nodded. "The house thing is what makes the parole officer's information good news. First off, all the evidence points to Teddy as the one who nabbed Maggie. Second, Trevor believes that's the *only* place Teddy has to go, so..."

"That's where he has her, Jake. I want to go to that house, Jake. I want you and me to go with baseball bats and blow torches and—"

She looked lost, completely bereft, and he knew that nothing he could say now would give her any reason to remain optimistic. Jake released her feet, and she didn't resist when he gently moved her knees to the side so that he could reach out and tuck the hair that had fallen in front of her face behind one ear. It was a move he'd used for fifteen years, one that soothed enough to calm her down.

But she jumped up and paced again. Jake thought about getting up and grabbing her but knew it was hopeless. He sat patiently, wishing he hadn't left his shot of bourbon on the desk.

The antique clock that Liz had insisted on bringing from their house on Long Island ticked away until the half hour when it released a single low bell. After another minute, she grabbed his glass and poured bourbon from the bar in with his earlier shots until the thing was almost filled to the brim. She returned to the loveseat and carefully sat down so as not to spill.

"I'm okay." Taking a gulp from his glass, she made a face and handed it to Jake. "When do you think you'll hear back from Trevor? Dammit, you know he has to tell Angie. Maggie was the Maid of Honor at their wedding."

"I'm sure he will." He took a gulp from the glass and then bent over, setting it on the floor. Resituating himself, he tugged Liz against him, wrapping an arm around her shoulders. "You know there's a silver lining in all of this."

"Oh, Jake. You don't get to play the Pollyanna part in this family. That's my job." She swiped her tears with open hands and turned to look up at him with a question-mark expression. "I can't see anything good about this."

"Well—" He looked down and saw that she was listening but that she was also ready to jump up again. "At least you're going to get one of your Christmas wishes and another gold star on that HEA wall chart of yours."

"Hmm. How's that?"

"Apparently, Maggie and Coop are together."

CHAPTER TWENTY

The Hunt

Trevor liked his job because he loved a mystery. The crimes themselves gave rise to a more visceral reaction. First, sadness, then anger. A lot of anger. But what drew him to police work? The reason he'd left a career in financial management, thus remaining a great disappointment to his father? That was the whodunit. The gathering of evidence. The hunt.

And he was hunting now because the search warrant that was executed on Teddy Amato's house—correction, the scumbag's deceased mother's house—didn't produce Maggie. It also failed to uncover the kind of information he needed to *find* Maggie. His frustration at her not being captive in the house was palpable. Worse was that Teddy Amato was not there either.

He'd moved her, but where?

Trevor had made a cursory list from the search that *would* be useful in getting a judge to sign off on an arrest warrant. They found florist receipts, rose petals, and some stems that matched similar items on the floor of Maggie's coat closet. Also, the dumb shit had left fingerprints in the apartment: on the door knob and a glass. At the very least, they had plenty of reasons to book the jerk *if* they could find him.

Correction, Trev. When we find her.

And that was the issue now. Teddy Amato could be anywhere within New York City's three hundred and four square land miles. Worse, he could have left the state. So—where was Teddy? It reminded him of the title of a book his toddler daughter loved. Trevor was sorry he couldn't remember the name.

He sighed and once again checked his notes on his desk, double-checking he'd not missed anything.

"Hey, there."

The interruption in his wandering thoughts was exactly what Trever needed to refocus. "Marcus. Something new?"

"Not much." His partner stood fidgeting with a manila folder. Marcus Brown was a good cop. A bulldozer of a man, he got extra points just for largess. As his Major Crimes partner of the last three years, Trevor had come to trust the man's instincts and, more to the point, appreciate his size.

"But something, right?" Trevor reached his hand up to take the folder and its contents.

"Photos from Amato's house. Place is like hoarder central or something. Even the mother's clothes are still there, all over the place, on hangers. Hell, according to our information, she's been dead, like, six years or something. Oh, and there's paper bags filled with paper bags. Weird."

"Okay, I get the idea." Trevor opened the folder and began turning over pictures, one at a time. "What about tangible evidence?"

"Besides what that editor, um, Cooper, right? Cooper said in his witness statement we can't even be sure Amato's got the woman. We have proof he was in her apartment, and the connection between the flowers in her closet and the stems, sheers, et cetera, in his house. He was pretty casual about fingerprints. But you knew that, so no, not much. Except, like I said, the mom's is a mess. We still have two CSIs combing through stuff."

Trevor wanted to throw something, but it would accomplish nothing, and they didn't have time for bullshit. "We have to have physical evidence, something that could prove Maggie Reynolds *was* there, that she was held there at some point. Where else could he have taken her?" He didn't have to verbalize his concerns, and the look on his partner's face confirmed it. They both knew it. The first day had been somewhat productive, but not enough. "Dammit." Even people without law enforcement connections knew the first forty-eight hours were critical.

His fist came down hard on the folder that offered little help in finding Maggie Reynolds. "Twenty-nine hours, Marcus. It's too long not to have some effing clue on where she is." If Maggie wound up dead… He put the thought into the back of his mind. What they needed now was to find Amato.

"Lab's running some other prints from the vic's apartment, but as to the perp's house? It's a bitch. There's thousands of items crammed in there, and an equal number of prints on everything. At least there's nothing to suggest Ms. Reynolds was ever injured in the dead mom's house, no blood or anything."

Trevor had looked at the clock maybe five minutes earlier, but he looked again.

Marcus sat down across from Trevor. Like a lot of squad room set-ups, their mutual desks were shoved against each other, their computers and landlines sharing sockets in the floor between them. "We're on empty, Trev."

"I know." Trevor finger-combed his hair from the forehead back, hoping something would pop into his brain. "You said that Teddy's place was some kind of hoarder's paradise, and we're still going over it?"

"Like I said, no holds barred."

The phone on Trevor's desk rang, and he grabbed it. "Caldwell."

"Detective Caldwell? It's Nick Cooper."

"Hey, Mr. Cooper." They'd spoken once before, and he wanted to put the man at ease, so he offered using a more personal address. "Feel free to call me Trev."

"Okay. Thanks. I don't want to disturb your efforts, but I'm going a little crazy here. Any word?"

"Not much, Mr. Cooper, we've got…"

"It's Nick, please. I'm told your wife is a friend of Maggie's, so it's personal for both of us."

"Okay, Nick. For now—I'll probably go back to the formal address in the event of anything public, like a press conference."

"You think it will come to that?"

"Well, Ms. Reynolds—uh, Maggie, she's been missing over twenty-four hours now. We may reach out for help from the public, we have a viable suspect and..."

"Yes, but isn't there a danger that he'd..."

It was Trevor's turn to interrupt. "Hurt her, or worse? Yes. There are circumstances when releasing information about a suspect escalates the timeline of the perp's intentions."

"And?"

"Listen, Nick. I know you're pacing the floors, and that only gets worse with each minute that passes, but you have to let us do our jobs." *How many times have I said that?* Trevor could play out too many scenarios in which letting the public have information too soon had a bad result; he shuddered to think of that happening to Maggie. "I wish I had better news, but we're going over Amato's place with a magnifying glass."

"I'm sure you are. I got a taste for your department's thoroughness when your CSIs started collecting evidence at Maggie's apartment."

"Thanks." Trevor was thinking of ways to sign off but remembered one of his rules: sometimes, people just didn't realize how much the smallest seemingly insignificant detail would matter. "While I have you, have you thought of anything new?"

"Maybe. First, thanks for clearing up some details Maggie had yet to share with me about Teddy Amato."

"No problem, but go on, Nick."

"It dawned on me—do you have all the letters?"

"You mean the letters shoved under Maggie's door?"

"No. There were two letters before I met Maggie."

"Explain, please."

"We had a substitute carrier for a week or so, and I guess that person figured to just leave 'em at my door because I was the newest tenant. I checked with some of the tenants on the floor but hadn't had a chance to ask Maggie. When our regular carrier came back on route, I showed them to her, and she took them back. Full disclosure?" Nick took a breath. "One more was delivered to my apartment, but you have it already because that envelope I *did* deliver to Ms. Reynolds."

"And that last one was your regular mail person? Even after you showed her the wrongly delivered mail earlier?"

"I get your inference, but those carriers have a lot of mail to deliver, and I'd venture a guess that a lot of that's by rote."

Trevor closed his eyes, trying to remember the USPS rules on dead letters. "Makes sense, but do you know your regular carrier's name?"

"It's Nancy. Don't know her last name, but she's apparently been on this route for several years. It seems like you would have the resources to track her down."

"And the letters didn't name Maggie as the addressee?"

"Well, the last one that came to me was to M. Amato and the building address. It had the floor noted but no apartment number." Trevor heard the slow intake of breath on the other end of the line. "That's why I gave that one to Maggie; a wild guess, really, because of the 'M.'"

"Then how'd Teddy get the right number to deliver the roses?"

"Somewhere along the way, Teddy must have found out more details on Maggie's whereabouts. That would make sense because the last letter I know Maggie received was shoved under the door. There was 'M. Amato' printed on the envelope, which we all know now is Maggie."

"Okay, all right, let me get on this, Nick. Maybe something will come of it." Trevor didn't expect anything more and was ready to hang up, but he remembered something Nick had said. He switched the phone to his other ear and laid his pen on the desk. "Hey, Nick. It seemed like you felt there was something else? Besides the letters."

"I did, and I'm actually feeling guilty about it."

"Why?" Trevor couldn't imagine what Nick Cooper had to feel guilty about, and it made him wonder if they were too hasty in dismissing him as a suspect. But then they had Jake Willis vouching for the guy, still—

"It's information. Maggie shared it with me the night she was taken."

Trevor switched ears again and flipped a paperclip at Marcus to get his attention. Motioning for his partner to pick up the line, he turned his attention back to the conversation with Nick. "So, it's not tangible evidence, then?"

"Well, yes, and no," Nick said. "I don't have the actual documents, but it's something that Maggie revealed to me, and at first it seemed so personal…"

"Listen, Nick," Trevor said, cutting him off. "Nothing can be personal in a case like this. Any little piece of information you have can be vital, no matter how irrelevant it may seem to you."

"I know. It's not so much what Maggie told me. It was…it's more about the end result that comes from her opening up to me."

Trevor realized that the two must have shared something intensely personal. After all, Nick had been clobbered in her apartment in the middle of the night. There'd been two glasses on the nightstand next to her bed, and, well, the bed was a mess. Whatever conclusions he wanted to draw as a detective, the human element was obvious. "Nick?"

"Sorry. I'm here. Have you pulled the divorce papers from Maggie's marriage to Ricky Amato? I think it was final about four years ago."

"No, but why would we?"

"Because Ricky and Teddy were brothers. They shared everything. And Maggie said their mother had acted for all the world that she was poor and crazy. Except, according to Maggie, the mother had a property, a brownstone, in Bay Ridge. She didn't say much else. It was kind of an aside."

"Kind of an aside? Come on, Nick. Think."

"Well, I did, and that's when it came to me. When she mentioned the property, it was really in passing. She said something like, 'And it's too bad I didn't fight Ricky for a piece of that place near the river, right?' I mean, it was almost like a joke. I realized this afternoon: if the Amatos inherited the property, the divorce paperwork would probably list the property by address in terms of a disposition."

Marcus quit listening in on the call, putting the receiver down gently in its cradle. He scribbled a big note and held it up for Trevor to see: GOING TO D.A. FOR SDT ON THE DIVORCE DOCS.

"Nick. Thanks. We've been grasping at straws on where Teddy might have Maggie stashed. This might be a dead end, but we're on it." Trevor ended the phone call to grab his Glock from the drawer and shove it into his shoulder harness, then slammed his arms into his coat and ran after Marcus. Time to track down an ADA and a judge and hopefully bring this bastard down.

CHAPTER TWENTY-ONE

Captive

Why the hell did she smell Italian food? The better question might have been, where the hell was she? Then Maggie remembered waking up before with the realization she was on the Amato brother's mother's property that sat two blocks from the waterfront in Bay Ridge. She'd only been there a few times when she was with Ricky.

She'd loved him heart and soul in the beginning. Even if it meant dinner with his disapproving mother and Teddy. Mostly, it had been in the older brownstone on Pacific in the Boerum Hill neighborhood. A place that had become increasingly impossible to visit. Not only because Maggie couldn't always hide Ricky's blows but because his mother had become a hoarder. In the year Maggie filed for divorce, she could barely navigate the hallway to the powder room off the kitchen.

Hell, she wasn't welcome there anyway. Not once she'd refused to defend Ricky's illegal activities. Now it appeared Teddy was using the almost-waterfront place to do his dirty deeds.

Her mind was still dulled by whatever Teddy had used to knock her out, despite the earlier chat they'd had and the pain burning at her wrists.

Oh, God, Coop.

Coop back at her place, on the floor, immobile. She remembered moving toward him when she heard Teddy Amato snarl, "Don't move, bitch." Then everything had gone dark.

She looked down at herself. She was wearing some old jeans and an Aerosmith sweatshirt from the clothes Teddy had thrown at her before he locked the door on his last visit. The clothes smelled like moth balls, and the room was cold. She shivered, doubting the heat had been on in years.

It registered she wasn't in her running shorts. She swallowed hard to keep from puking. Holding her breath long enough to work through the fact of Teddy touching her, dressing her, and that she must have passed out again after his last visit, it gave her a different kind of chill.

She shook it off, knowing she needed to focus on the present. "Okay, Mags, think." Talking aloud to herself felt like company.

One window. It was covered with a blind, but somebody had left the slats partway open, and there were red and orange ribbons of color interspersed with the dusky blue sky. The colors indicated sunset, and so it had to be a west-facing window. Bingo. She was in one of the bedrooms that had matching gabled windows over a covered front porch.

Teddy must have cut the ties to dress her, but her hands were bound again.

If she could get the zip ties free, she had a chance.

There was no choice but to try and escape. They'd never find her here, not unless Teddy left pixie dust. And Teddy wasn't in this gig for ransom. He only wanted one thing—Maggie Amato, nee Reynolds, dead.

The key turned in the lock, and despite the fact that she'd been working the zip ties that bound her hands against a bolt that stuck out from the old metal bed frame, she still wasn't free.

She also wasn't sure if she was strong enough to run. And she had to be.

Because when the opportunity arrived, she was going to have to jump at it.

CHAPTER TWENTY-TWO

The Warrant

Trevor Caldwell was barking orders to a handful of men, all preparing for the raid on the Bay Ridge property that was now the subject of their manhunt for Teddy Amato. Nick was seated on a chair in a far corner. Whether Caldwell wanted him to or not, wherever they were headed, he was going.

For Maggie.

The search warrant had been issued maybe an hour earlier, and Trevor had spent that time coordinating with the 68th Precinct for the raid. Nick had been involved since the warrant that produced Maggie's divorce documents. He'd been right—the pillow talk from two nights ago had coughed up the vital information that Teddy and Ricky Amato had inherited a Bay Ridge property from their mother. The property was still in her maiden name, hence why they hadn't spotted it before.

Of course, he was eavesdropping, which was why he knew he had to intervene soon, or he'd be left in the dust. He sat up straighter as Trevor approached.

"You know where she is." A statement of fact. Nick stood, using his height to advantage over the slightly shorter detective.

"Yes," Trevor said. "Good chance anyway, and thanks. It's evident from the divorce documents that the Amatos inherited their mom's second home in Bay Ridge. Looks like it's been in the family forever. We followed the title search, and Rose Amato inherited the property from her father. We had a plain-clothes walk the block this afternoon, and she said the trash can was full in the driveway. It's not much, but the last thing we want to do is spook the creep."

Nick knew what to expect, which didn't matter. "I'm going."

"Like hell you are, Mr. Cooper. You're not."

"I guess this is that point where the familiar 'Nick' is put aside. You're the cop, and I'm a civilian."

"That sums it up, sir."

"Yes. Except I'm still going. You wouldn't have this lead without me, Detective."

"And we're thankful, but it doesn't change the fact that I'm not taking a civilian along to serve a search warrant in a potential hostage situation."

"I have the address, Caldwell."

"So what? You going to show up, help us out somehow? You can only make it worse."

"I don't agree."

"Don't make me lock you up, Cooper."

"You don't know Maggie. I do. If she's not"—Nick paused and took a calming breath—"dead already, she's figuring some way out, an escape. Do you even know the history she has with Amato?"

"I know she was married to Ricky Amato, a smalltime hood and rocker. I know about her disbarment, and…"

Nick interrupted. "Not disbarment. She withdrew from the practice of law."

"Same thing."

"No, Detective, it's not. She could have fought the disbarment. She could have hidden behind her absolute right to attorney–client privilege. And if she had? Ricky Amato might still be in business. She gave herself up and let the feds push the whole conspiracy crap on her. She gave you guys evidence without the benefit of any in-turn protections."

"I get it, Cooper. She's one of the good guys. It doesn't mean you get some kind of pass to get you or one of *my* people killed."

"That is unlikely. And besides, I'm licensed to carry…"

"I don't give a rat's ass about your CCW permit, Cooper, not to mention the myriad nightmare scenarios of you going whacko on Teddy Amato. I'm not taking you on a warrant serve. Especially this one."

Nick stayed toe to toe with Caldwell. He wasn't intentionally intimidating, but he had three inches on the guy, and his shoulders were broader. "Okay, don't take me along. But I'll be there, Detective. You can't stop me from being there."

"Damn you, Nick. It's police business, period. I'm not having some civilian go all *Mortal Kombat* on me. Stay put."

The detective's frustration was evidenced by his falling back to the familiar of "Nick," but he hid it and walked away, barking more orders. The room emptied except for a clerk and a handful of law enforcement officers assigned to other matters.

Nick talked to himself. "Screw police business. This is Maggie. *My Maggie.*"

Saying it to the walls hit Nick. The admission, still new, continued to catch him off guard. It felt like he'd stuck his finger in a socket. He was not going to find love and lose it in less than forty-eight hours.

Thinking it to himself or saying it aloud, it didn't matter. It was freedom from Meg, from the loss. Oh, Meg was still in his head. She always would be. Hell, Emily was a daily reminder of her mother. But somehow, now there was room for Maggie.

What about Emily, Nick?

He knew he was responsible for his daughter, knew that he shouldn't risk leaving Emily without a parent, knew he wasn't Rambo in a book editor's clothing. Even if it was to save Maggie.

But Nick had to do something.

He crossed the room and punched the elevator button, hitting the "B" for Basement and his car. He'd think of something.

CHAPTER TWENTY-THREE

Coop on Board

Nick beat Caldwell and his warrant team to the house. He didn't imagine by much, but he was still there first and had found his way along a side yard, looking for a place to get into the two-story structure. The house needed work, reinforcing the information that Teddy Amato was now, and had been for some time, the dwelling's sole owner.

His concern at present was ingress and doing so closest to Maggie's proximity. If the house was true to a standard brownstone design, the bedrooms were all upstairs. The living room would be large, and the kitchen and dining areas, probably a small added bath, would occupy the entire downstairs. He'd already tried a window on the side of the house that must access the basement. It was nailed shut.

He doubted Teddy would hold Maggie on the first floor. Even if he did, Nick had already decided that entering the house on the second floor gave him an advantage. That meant getting in through an upstairs window, locating Maggie, and getting her out of there.

The air was cooling off, and clouds were rolling in from the northwest. He zipped up his parka, more to keep it from catching on something than to protect himself from the cold.

Nick was no stranger to weapons, and he patted the Glock in his pocket. He was also no stranger to action. He'd been twenty-two when the Twin Towers came down. His inactive-duty status post—four ROTC years at Cornell—had ended with his June graduation, leaving him subject to being called to duty under an Individual

Ready Reserve commitment. He could have been called up. He wasn't. So he signed up and did two tours in Afghanistan.

Standing in the shadow of the house, he saw a black car drive by. No sirens, no lights; Caldwell would set up with stealth. Nick thought it was a scout car, feeding information to Caldwell. Once everyone was in place, the SWAT team would use skill and stealth to be in place to break the door down, all without Teddy Amato's knowledge. The detective would be right with them.

He watched as the black car kept moving, heading east. Nick figured that gave him anywhere from five to ten minutes, max. He moved around to the back yard with cover from the darkness. A light was now on in the back of the house. Nick figured it for the kitchen.

His watch hands were dead on seven p.m.

If he had faith in some higher power, now would've been the time for its application.

And there it was, a ladder. It was tilted against the back wall of the house, and if it wasn't broken, would get Nick up on the sloped roof that ran across the front porch. Once there, he'd have access to both windows that faced west.

It was risky because he'd be vulnerable to any and all approaching the house from the street.

But it was Maggie. No risk was too great.

He moved fast, hugging the ladder to his side and then leaning it against the ridge of the porch roof on the east side of the house. He heard a cat cry next door and a trash can lid clatter to the ground. Nick held his breath. After a ten-second count, he moved again. Noting a missing rung on the ladder's bottom, he put his full weight on the second, letting out a low whistle when it held.

Nick was up and lying prone on the roof in a matter of seconds. He lay still and in shadow for a full minute. The black car rolled slowly back down the street from the other direction, and he believed its presence would be the move signal for a go in terms of Caldwell's team, which meant now or never for Nick.

A light switched on in the window to his left.

Bingo.

He had no choice now. Nick rose to a stoop position and moved.

CHAPTER TWENTY-FOUR

Coop & Teddy

Teddy loomed over Maggie. In the moment, with the light behind him, he could have been Ricky. Brothers. At some point, Rose Amato's boys, fifteen months apart, must have been normal. Maybe happy, playful kids, just like other boys their ages.

But that had changed, and Maggie had firsthand knowledge of their evil bent. She had no doubt that Teddy intended to kill her; if not that, then to cause major bodily injury, no doubt scars for life.

It couldn't happen. She wouldn't let it. She had seen her future with Coop in one magic night and refused to let it go.

A handful of hours had equaled a lifetime in her heart. She loved him. And she loved Emily. And because of them and the last two months, she'd risen above the ashes of her past. Like some living illusion to a phoenix. She smiled to herself, wondering what Coop would think of her literary genius.

"Wipe that smile off your face. I can't believe my brother ever saw anything in you. You're such a skinny bitch." Teddy laughed, which Maggie found so unfunny. "You're like some basketball player with boobs. Oh, right, except you don't have any. You know my brother could have had any hot babe he wanted?"

Maggie figured it was Teddy's best way to belittle her, to hint at Ricky's having a bunch of groupies wanting him toward the end. *Surprise, Teddy. I knew.* That Ricky had started sleeping around at some point toward the end of their relationship was no surprise. Of course he would, his head being even more inflated by his growing fame and the women that'd flocked around the band.

She'd seen them. Full-bodied, tattooed, half-dressed. She never got the nose ring thing, but the rest? Why wouldn't Ricky dabble? What bothered her the most was that one of their last times together had left her pregnant.

Maggie hated herself for believing *now* that losing that baby was the best thing possible. Teddy snorted, and she returned her attention to her captor.

"Whatever he saw in me is moot," she said. "He certainly didn't care for me."

"Wrong." Teddy yelled the word. It felt like she'd landed in some kind of game show, and every time she was incorrect as far as Teddy was concerned, a big buzzer would go off and end with him yelling a single word, like now. "Wrong. Wrong. Wrong."

"Really? Okay, well, I guess beating a woman to a pulp on a regular basis is how you Amato boys show your love."

"Bitch. Bitch. Bitch."

"Hmm. Welcome to the Department of Redundancy Department."

"What's that supposed to mean?"

"Oh, I don't know, Teddy. Maybe if I give you enough time, you'll be able to figure it out."

He stepped toward her, and Maggie knew she'd gone too far. Trying to spar tit for tat with a limited intellect was pointless, and given the man's proclivity for violence and the fact he hated her guts, she might have just sealed her fate. She scrunched back against the metal bed frame, the springs in the ancient mattress squeaking like a thousand mice. When she pushed hard to make herself smaller, she felt the zip tie push further against the bolt.

Almost there.

Teddy stopped at the end of the bed. "You killed my brother."

"I didn't, Teddy. Some violent felon on the same cell block either didn't like Ricky or somebody on the outside wanted him dead and paid for that guy to do it. But me? Nothing I did leading up to that point was the cause of Ricky's death."

She knew her statements were bouncing off Teddy, that there was nothing she could do to change his mind. And that was when she saw a flash of his gun reflected from the overhead light in the room.

***

Nick had to act, and he didn't want to go in through the window with the light because there was a chance Teddy would be in and out of there without rhyme or reason. First, he had to check the darkened window. Maybe it wasn't even open.

It was.

He tugged gently, and the window budged. It was stiff, though, and he needed to pull it hard, which meant the possibility of noise. He took a deep breath, and it moved further. In another two minutes, he was in, standing in a lightless room, waiting for his eyes to adjust.

He shielded his phone with one hand and turned on the flashlight. *Damn.* It seemed super bright, but he only needed seconds to assess furniture, boxes, and stuff in the way of a clear path to the door. He shut the light off and stepped carefully, based on the memory of his quick assessment.

Cobwebs attached to his face and hair as he took another step. He brushed at them, cursing under his breath, stepping further toward the bedroom door.

All that mattered was Maggie. Except it wasn't true. He was out here, maybe on a fool's errand, and he had a child. A motherless daughter. He had no right to endanger his life for anyone other than Emily.

No. Not true.

Maggie mattered.

The pounding of his heart was surely loud enough to alert Teddy to his presence as if Poe himself were increasing the crescendo of each beat, giving Nick away.

He took a deep breath, then heard a loud crash from the room next door.

Nick jumped into action.

***

Teddy was obviously pissed. "Bitch, super bitch. You've got a smart mouth, Maggie. But don't try to confuse me. I'm not stupid, stupid." He moved closer toward the bed.

She was numb yet wanted to laugh out loud. What the hell did "stupid, stupid" equal?

"You skinny slut. You don't think I know what you been doing with that editor guy? You're all alike, and you're the worst. You broke Ricky's heart, and they took everything from him, all his rock and roll money. The effing feds even took his guitars and shit, froze them as, as…"

Despite her circumstances, Maggie couldn't resist. "Assets."

He waved the gun at her again. "You smart-mouthed whore. Maybe you'd like to find out just how much like Ricky I can be?" He grabbed his crotch with one hand, gyrating his hips.

Maggie's terror returned. It was worse than when she'd heard something accompanied by high-pitched squeaks and the sound of claws clicking across the hardwood floor earlier.

Rats.

It made her thank God for the horrid bed and the bars that held her hands captive. Anything not to be on the floor.

Teddy made another sexually provocative move, and she was glad her stomach was empty so she couldn't vomit. She watched him while carefully continuing to wiggle the zip tie against the screwhead that stuck out from the metal headboard.

It snapped, and it took all of her energy to keep her arms from flying out from behind her due to the force of the release and at the prospect of freedom. *Breathe, Mags. Breathe, dammit. Don't let him know you're free.* Feeling was rushing back into her fingers, and the tingling made her want to shake her arms about. She bit her lip, tasting blood.

"Yeah. Yeah. That's what I should do. I can *be* Ricky for you, skinny Reynolds. I can make you feel like an Amato again." He took another two steps toward the bed.

Maggie was wrong. She could vomit. She swallowed hard, the taste in her mouth awful.

Sirens? There were sirens. But when weren't there in New York City? Didn't matter what borough, what section of the city, sirens were an everyday, every minute kind of thing.

Teddy twisted his neck. He'd heard them too but didn't seem phased. He took another step in Maggie's direction, the gun still in his hand, his grin disgusting. And now she could smell him. Rank, no shower? If the heat wasn't on, as she suspected, he wouldn't be able to shower anyway. And alcohol. So that was where he was getting his courage. Maybe he wouldn't be able to get it up.

"I'm warning you, Teddy. You can't rely on your stereotype of women." She figured he didn't even know what a stereotype was, but she wanted to keep bantering, keep him occupied. "I won't go down without a fight. Your brother taught me that."

Her mentioning Ricky seemed to give him pause because he'd been coming at her like a cat and now stalled his approach, watching her like she was a bird sitting on a low-hanging feeder waiting to be snatched.

She could imagine his pouncing, his arms on her, his mouth coming toward hers, his forcing her legs apart—

She held her breath and readied herself to react, to kick, claw, bite, knee him, whatever it took. The sirens sounded closer.

***

Nick had been listening at the door. He knew Caldwell's assault would come straight down Colonial Road. They hadn't come in silent at first, but the sirens stopped, and he figured that put the rescue team a block away. He'd seen the black car come from the direction of Fort Hamilton Athletic Field, slowing half a block away and coming to a halt right before he'd ducked in the window.

He didn't have much time, and whether Caldwell's group would break into the house any second, he didn't care. He kicked open the door to the room.

Nick saw it in slow motion: Maggie leaping off the bed, flailing her arms in every direction. It seemed she was making every conceivable move she knew to do damage to Teddy.

Despite being thin, Teddy was sinewy, and he managed to kick back. Hard. Maggie went down. And then Nick saw Teddy's gun.

He saw Teddy's arm come up and the gun aimed. A direct hit on Maggie if the jerk fired.

Nick leaped simultaneously with the crack of the weapon.

He was on top of Teddy on the floor, rolling over and over until they hit the wall on the other side of the room. He had no idea where Maggie was, whether she'd been hit.

And if hell hadn't already broken loose, it did when two SWAT team members burst through the window, and Teddy's body was suddenly airborne. Detective Caldwell had entered through the door at the precise same moment. The team members had Teddy in a lock, but not for long. There were more officers behind Caldwell, and they whisked Teddy away.

Nick sat up, trying to find Maggie.

"Let me go, dammit. Let me get to Coop." God, he loved her voice.

She was on her knees next to him, but suddenly he felt weak, and pain set in his lower back, on his right side. A lot of pain. And then things started going numb.

"Damn you, Coop, damn you," she said. "I was handling things just fine."

"Sure you were, honey." Nick hadn't used that word in over two years. He had a sudden thought: *I hope it's okay, Meg. That I'm using that word again.*

He heard Caldwell barking for the ambulance and Maggie's voice babbling about his being stupid and that she loved him—*That's cool*, he thought—and that it was all her fault. *No, it wasn't.*

But he couldn't answer anybody. Not his name, not his date of birth, not if he could feel his legs, which he couldn't. No matter what they asked, his mouth refused to operate.

He was thinking he'd have to find a way to make everything up to Maggie, for blowing their first day together. He'd been making plans when she'd fallen asleep against his chest. Making all kinds of plans as he felt her breath on his skin with each exhale. And how they'd tell Emily.

And then the world went blank.

CHAPTER TWENTY-FIVE

Maggie vs. Coop

The first week, Maggie was at Coop's bedside in the hospital. The stupid man had taken a bullet meant for her, and after cursing him every which way, she'd advanced to heartfelt entreaties to whatever universe was out there to let him pull through.

After learning the nurse's schedules and when they had shift changes, she'd managed to sneak in Emily once. Maggie had spoken with Emily, told her what to expect, but she hadn't realized how mature Emily really was. She should have known, should have understood that Emily had already been exposed to death. She'd been there when her mom got sick and then died.

But losing another parent? That was not in the cards for this tough little girl. Emily had tiptoed in with Maggie. She'd stood by her father's bed, lightly rubbing the top of his hand, the one with the least amount of IVs, repeating, "It's okay, Daddy. I'm here. Reynolds is here." She whispered it over and over. The "Reynolds" part touched Maggie.

Coop didn't look as bad after the first few days, but he was still too out of it to know they were there. If he did, he didn't let on.

Although the bullet was removed, it had clipped his liver and smashed by his spine. There was significant nerve trauma, and the doctors wouldn't yet commit to whether he'd walk again.

Coop would be okay. He had to be. Never in her life had Maggie felt so connected to anyone. The secrets of her childhood, her past, she had kept to herself. Only Liz knew, and now Maggie wanted to share it all.

To tell Coop about the way her father had beaten her mother and threatened Maggie. She'd seen marital violence firsthand, and you'd think she would have learned, and Ricky's first assault should have been enough to send her packing.

But it hadn't.

At least she wouldn't have to deal with it over the holidays because Teddy's trial had been put over until after the New Year. She didn't think she cared anymore. Of course, she'd have to testify. Still, the only thing that mattered to her in that regard was that Teddy was sent to prison for-freaking-ever.

Even more than that? She wanted Coop to wake up. He had to, and then they'd be fine.

***

When Coop's hospital stay went beyond two weeks, he was placed in a physical rehabilitation center, and besides the fact that Coop was still uncommunicative, Maggie lost touch even more. Because of the extended stay, Emily moved in with Liz and Jake.

Halloween came and went, and Maggie had taken great joy in trick or treating in Liz and Jake's building with all the Willis children and Emily. She'd asked Liz about Coop, but the answers were guarded. Yes, he was awake, not in a coma, and yes, he was in physical therapy. No, he hadn't asked to see Maggie.

Liz had never been evasive with Maggie, *not ever* in their long friendship. That she had become so now was beyond disconcerting. It left her to conclude that Coop despised her. She was, after all, the reason he'd been shot.

Sometimes, Maggie felt desperate, and she'd open the peephole of her door because she thought she heard a noise. Other times, she'd hear someone in the hallway and the door open to Coop's apartment, but it would be Emma, the cleaning lady. She came once a week and kept the place shipshape for Coop and Emily's return.

Teaching filled a lot of the emptiness Maggie felt, especially as the holidays approached. There was a lot to be done to finalize the winning Christmas story and how it would be presented at the school pageant at the end of the second week in December.

Almost every week, Liz would call ahead, and they'd visit when she picked up fresh clothes for Coop.

"He still hasn't asked for me?" Maggie asked.

Liz smiled her *"Patience, Maggie"* smile. She sat on the sofa with her and held Maggie's hand until, as usual, Maggie would swipe at the tears slipping down her face, trying to be reassured by Liz's words, like, "He's not walking yet," or, "The therapy is full-time," and, "The doctors are optimistic, but he's a man. It's that stupid thing they do, you know. Nobody sees any weakness, nobody gets inside."

Maggie listened to her friend's pep talks, but it did no good, and she responded in the same way to what felt like just so much rhetoric. "That's not true of Coop, I just know it. He doesn't want to see me because it's my fault, Lizzie. It's all my fault."

"Knock it off, Maggie. It's not your fault."

This same conversation continued for weeks, whether they met for lunch or spoke on the phone, but by November, Maggie had given up. She didn't want to see Liz, the kids, or Emily. Especially Emily.

What would Coop's daughter think of her now?

Maggie had conversations with Emily and Coop. Imaginary discussions, like Harvey's rabbit: "I'm so sorry, Em," and, "I'm so sorry, Coop. It's all my fault."

She also had the "everything's okay" talk with herself, the "world's ending" rants, the "Coop hates me" blubbering, and then, when she'd let everything go for the time being, she'd be okay.

That was how she made it to Thanksgiving.

Then the dream of Maggie and Coop having this special time together disappeared, the imagined moments popped like bubbles off the end of one of those little plastic wands.

Liz had been angry when Maggie refused the invitation to Thanksgiving dinner at the Willis home. And it became a battle royal at Christmastime. They'd met for lunch at their favorite deli the Saturday before school let out. Maggie had brought all the presents she had for Emily and the Willis children, plus a bottle of wine and a set of fun Christmas towels for her thoroughly-Christmas-freak best friend. The last item had been wrapped like a book, and the label noted: "To Coop, Happy Holidays, Maggie."

"I'm not taking these gifts, Mags," Liz had said. "I'm not. You need to come to my house and deliver them in person."

"How is Coop, and will he be there?"

"That's a compound question, which you of all people should know, and beside the point. I won't take no for an answer." Liz had remained deliberately evasive in almost every conversation about Coop since he went to rehab.

The worst part of it was her best friend *knew* Coop was avoiding Maggie. Knew and wouldn't cop to it. That Liz, of all people, kept shielding her from the truth—Coop hated Maggie. He didn't want to see her, and whatever they'd had was over. She was numb.

She'd shaken off the thoughts, realizing Liz was speaking.

"My children have seen you every Christmas of their lives, and Emily misses you."

"Does Emily even care about me, Liz? Really? It's been almost two months. I haven't seen her since Halloween. Her dad's all screwed up because of me, and she's been yanked from everything she knew and loved. Let's not forget, ah, her mother dying and all, two years earlier."

"Oh, come on, Maggie. This is a pity party if ever I've seen one."

"Really? Then how come you won't answer my question?"

"Which one?"

Maggie had taken a deep breath, hating to fight with her best friend. She'd pushed anyway. "Will Nick be there for Christmas?" She'd started calling him Nick because Coop himself seemed an unattainable dream right now.

"You mean Coop?"

"Cut it out, Lizzie. Obtuse doesn't become you."

Liz had let out a heavy sigh. "I know. I'm sorry. Yes, he'll be there for Christmas Eve and Day. He's staying in the guest room. We sprung him."

"From rehab. So, he's still not walking." Maggie couldn't explain the ache that overwhelmed her. She could barely breathe, and once again, tears had threatened to spill over and make a mess of her face.

"He's getting around in his wheelchair just fine. He's also walking some in therapy."

"What does that mean? Walking some."

"You know those parallel bars in the Olympics? Well, it's like that: they help him up, and then he uses the support of the bars to walk. It's slow, but he's improving all the time." Liz had reached out and touched Maggie's hand. Maggie hadn't pulled back. She couldn't lose Liz too. "You know, you could make an appointment to visit."

The shock of Liz's statement had broken the spell. "He doesn't *want* to see me."

"I think he does."

"Uh-huh, did you ask him?"

"No." Liz couldn't lie. Being evasive, she could manage. Flat out lying? Not so much.

"And once again, I rest my case. He hasn't said he wanted to see me to anyone, has he?"

"No."

Liz had looked crestfallen, and Maggie had so wanted to throw out a lifeline that she'd lied. "Okay. You take the presents; I'll pencil it in."

"No penciling. That's bullshit."

"Okay. All right. I'll be there for Christmas Day. I'm reading at St. Andrew's on Christmas Eve."

"Since when did you get religion?"

"Since I lost everything I loved."

Liz had let the comment go, and they'd somehow stumbled through the rest of their lunch, chattering about the mundane stuff. Maggie had barely made it home before she had a complete emotional breakdown. It wasn't just Nick, but she and her best friend forever had a wedge between them. It had become obvious when, despite the champagne they'd ordered, there was no outright laughter, no sillies, no stupid girlfriend stuff.

And what about her book editor from across the hall?

After crying for an hour, Maggie had put a few more ornaments on her little pine tree. It was real and in a pot that she was able to water daily. She'd even put some lights on it, and sometimes, at night, she'd fallen asleep on the sofa while watching the strings of white blink on and off.

Somehow, she'd made it through the Christmas pageant, and the story that won the award had been well received. And because she'd promised to be at the Willis's for Christmas Day, when Liz, Jake, the kids, and Emily, had shown for the pageant, everything was relaxed, no tension, and she *was* glad to finally see Emily. The girls had all been dressed up in red and green velvets; the boys had worn plaid pants, white shirts, and snap-on ties. Jake had looked distinguished and relaxed, and Liz had been radiant and as in love as ever.

What a wonderful night.

Maggie was ashamed about her lie, and although she'd again confirmed she'd come to the Willis's on Christmas Day, she'd had no intention of keeping that promise.

The week leading up to Christmas had been blasé, and she'd spent Christmas Day the same way as she had Thanksgiving: soup kitchens, helping at the church, a frozen turkey dinner, and a bottle of champagne. It was a split. Getting too stupid always ended in a self-pitying crying fit.

Liz's phone messages had gone from cheerful, "You're on your way, right?" to worried, "Maggie, are you there? Are you sick? What's up? Are you okay?" Eventually, the tone had become angry but subdued. Maggie had stopped listening at number seven.

She prayed they were happy, that Nick was enjoying his time with Emily and away from some dreary rehab center. That the presents and laughter were enough.

And when she finally fell asleep, she couldn't help thinking about the present for Nick. Did he like it? She rolled over, admitting to herself it didn't matter. She'd crippled him. It *was* her fault, no matter what they all said or tried to make her believe.

And as she had so many times in the last two months, Christmas ended with Maggie crying herself to sleep.

CHAPTER TWENTY-SIX

New Year's Eve

Maggie had told Liz for the one-hundredth time she wasn't going to Liz's New Year's Eve party. She'd managed the Thanksgiving holiday, and Christmas alone, and now she felt as though there was some light at the end of her tunnel other than sorrow and remorse.

And that was why she wasn't going to answer her phone now. It was Liz for the fourth time that morning. Truth? She wanted to go. She'd been saving a dress since an after-holidays sale last year. And why would she let the too-good-to-be-true, too-handsome-for-his-own-good Nick Cooper stop her?

Maggie picked up her cell phone. "Hello, Liz."

"Ah-hah! I knew I was in your phone book. You've known it was me every time I've called, Mags." Maggie knew the tone. Liz wasn't angry. She was faking.

"Sorry, friend. I've been a pill."

"I'm glad you agree. Now, it's time to knock it off and come to our party tonight. "Coop won't be at the party, Mags. There's no excuse for you *not* to come." Maggie was about to interject, but Liz cut her off. "And have you forgotten you owe me?"

"Lizzie." Maggie took a sip from the coffee she'd brewed in the present Liz ordered delivered to her apartment, which, although brought by messenger, had been dropped-off in an appropriate huff. Maggie was pretty sure Liz had asked the delivery person to be surly on purpose. "I don't like New Year's Eve. I never have." She ignored the "You owe me" remark completely.

"Oh, poppycock, Mags. And cripes, no whining. You've come to Christmas with us every year since you left Ricky. This would make four. And don't get technical—this New Year's Eve bash *is the same* as Christmas, except it's going to be huge."

"Okay. Okay. I give." She wanted Liz back on her side, in her life. And since the New Year meant resolutions, she needed to be honest with herself. Maggie wanted news of Nick, no matter how bad it was. Perhaps being at the party would allow her to get his status.

"Wow, really?" Liz said. Maggie waited, knowing Liz wasn't done. "All right, then. It's a deal. You can't let me down again, Maggie. I mean it."

"I won't. I am sorry about Christmas, Lizzie."

"I know you are."

***

The party was fabulous. Maggie had to admit she was having a good time. Still, even though she knew Nick wasn't going to be there, she kept looking, hoping that one time the front door to the apartment would open and in would come a handsome, tall, slightly greying, blue-eyed man with a brilliant smile, one just for her.

And he'd be standing, walking toward her. No paralysis.

She wasn't above being swept off her feet or living a fantasy. At least now, she could have the fantasy and not break down into a puddle of tears.

The champagne glass in her hand was almost empty, and although she shouldn't, she thought it was time for another glass. She waited, though, and looked out from Liz and Jake's balcony onto the city. She loved Christmas, and hated she'd missed it, but there was no point in continuing to beat herself up for being morose and stupid.

She felt the glass in her hand tip a little, realizing someone was pouring bubbly liquid to the brim.

"Don't turn around, Reynolds."

Her knees crumbled. She almost went down, but a strong arm grabbed her and rescued the glass. "Near sinful waste of really expensive shit, Mags."

It couldn't be Nick, Coop—it couldn't be. If she lost it and started to fall, was she going to wind up in his lap, in his wheelchair? *God, Coop. I'm so sorry it's all my fault.*

She started to turn around, but he stopped her. "Don't turn around. Not yet. I got stuff I need to say."

"That wasn't too articulate, Editor-man."

"No, probably not." She heard the smile in his tone. She wanted to see him, but he secured the glass in her hand from behind, and now his hands—*both hands*—held her in place at her waist. Could that happen if he was in a wheelchair? Was he standing? Maybe he was propped against a wall. What had he done with the bottle of champagne?

"I'm sorry, sweetheart. I've put you through hell." His tone was pleading, regretful.

"You think?"

"Oh, good. You haven't changed. I was counting on that."

"Oh, I've changed. I'm tougher than old jerky now." She wasn't going to melt simply because he was talking to her again. He didn't deserve it.

His laugh filled her up inside like nothing was wrong, but it had been. It had all been so very wrong. "And you've kept your sense of humor. I thought for sure you'd lose it given what I put you through."

"You didn't put me through anything, Nick."

"I must have for you to call me Nick."

"You're right. You did put me through a lot, you jerk." A lot? That didn't begin to express how horrid it had all been. She didn't understand. God, she wanted to, but her heart was just getting back to normal.

"I'm sorry."

She spun around, strong enough to escape his grasp. The shock of seeing him turned her legs into jelly. "You're sorry? Why should you be sorry? I'm the one that nearly got you killed. I'm the reason you're in a wheelchair…why you didn't want to see me."

His kiss stopped her diatribe. Then he stepped back. "So, so untrue." He swept his arms from his neck toward his feet. "And look. No chair."

"I see." She looked him up and down. Damn, but he was gorgeous. "What about everything I heard, and why didn't you call me? You broke my effing heart." Tears sprung, spilling down her face with abandon. "Damn it all to hell."

He took her face in his hands, and she tried tugging free of his hold.

"Mags." He let loose a low groan, his face shamed. "I know. And I'm sorry. I was weak. Weak in body, spirit, and mind. I was having a righteous want-to-die party. But, I didn't blame you for the shooting, Maggie. I never blamed you. It wasn't your fault, baby." He released his hold but not his earnestness. "It *was* wrong that I shut you out, made it so you didn't even want to see Em. I apologize. Neither of you deserved that. You needed each other, and I took that away from you."

Crud. *Baby.* How was she supposed to be righteously indignant if he was going to call her baby? He never had before. "Yes, you did. You made me believe it was all my fault."

"But it wasn't."

"Was too."

He kissed her forehead, and the words came out with his lips resting at her hairline, "It wasn't."

"Was."

He kissed her nose and stayed there, his breath feathering against her cheeks. "Not."

"I got you shot, Nick, whether you want to accept that or not. I. Got. You. Shot." She used her finger against his chest, pressing it into his sternum with each word.

He responded by kissing her ear. "You." Then her other ear. "Did." He kissed her neck. "Not." Then his mouth brushed lightly against her lips. "Get me shot."

He smelled like peppermint and that sage-brushy scent of his aftershave, subtle but sexy. It washed over her while she wondered what the heck her next move was supposed to be. She didn't want to disengage from him.

Not ever.

"You didn't show up for Christmas Day, Reynolds. That totally sucked."

"Since when do you say stuff like 'totally sucked'? And I couldn't be there. I couldn't see you, and you didn't want to see me."

They remained just inches apart from each other, their lips even closer. If the situation wasn't making her so freaking hot, Maggie would have laughed aloud. The champagne glass miraculously stayed in her hand, which was weird. For sure, she should have dropped it by now.

"I did want to see you. I was desperate to see you, so much so, silly girl, that I practically killed myself in therapy the week leading up to Christmas, and damned if I didn't walk, you hear me?" He tipped her chin up, ending the perpetual near kiss they'd been in for minutes. "I walked through Liz and Jake's front door on Christmas Eve, devastated at your absence. At least until I was reassured you were coming for Christmas Day."

"Shit."

"Now whose mastery of the English language is lacking?" He locked her gaze with his, and Maggie was failing. Her breathing was shallow, her heart pounding. Maybe she wasn't too young for a heart attack. "And can you imagine how disappointed I was when we all waited, and waited, and waited, and…"

"Well, why the hell didn't someone tell me?"

"Because I wanted to surprise you."

"No, it was a freakin' test. You were testing me, you jerk." When she realized the truth of it, she pulled back and tried again to escape.

"Maggie, stop it." He pulled her to him, crushing her against him. "I'd call you a little idiot, but you're not little. You're an Amazon. My Amazon, Reynolds. You might as well get used to it."

"Nobody owns me, Nick Cooper. Nobody."

"Oh, hell, will you knock it off? I'm trying to say something here."

She rested the side of her face against his chest, listening to his heart. But she'd be damned if she'd admit she loved him now. Motionless, she let her breathing settle into normal.

"Okay. Are you listening?" he asked.

"Maybe."

"I'll take that. Here it is: I was a monumental ass. I was petrified and scared, and I've never been physically weak in my life. It was not a pretty sight, and I couldn't—well, once I was cognitive again, and they moved me to physical rehab—I couldn't bring myself to see anyone."

"You saw Lizzie."

"Not in the beginning. She just had a list from me and then left the items with the nurse's station. I talked to her on the phone, though. I made her tell me everything about you, what you were doing, if you were okay."

She pushed away and stared up at him for a second. "So what'd Lizzie do, lie? Because I was *not* okay, Nick Cooper."

Coop pulled her back against his chest and said, "Don't move."

Oh, she was tempted to test him, but she didn't want to be away from the feel of him, so she stayed. Suddenly, his coat was around her shoulders. Maggie didn't notice that she'd become so cold she could barely talk without shivering. That was the problem with super-hot New Year's Eve dresses.

A thought flashed through her mind. Being in love was an effing dichotomy.

"Nobody lied," he said. "Well, not per se. I just wanted to do this. To show you and tell you myself."

Maggie looked up at Coop again. "And it's okay with everybody that I was completely devastated, totally crushed, absolutely miserable for weeks and weeks and wee…?"

An index finger against her mouth shushed her. "No, it wasn't all right at all." His tone was regretful and sad. "I made a gargantuan mess of things with everyone."

She pulled a hand back to punch him, but he caught it. Her other hand, remarkably, still held the glass of champagne. She stared at him, her chin up, and put the glass to her lips, downing the bubbly drink. "Well, you were *all* shits. Big, sneaky, lying, protective creeps."

He kissed her then, relentlessly. His hands holding her against him were her only means of support.

She drew back. Her gaze assessed his expressive face. God, she'd missed him. "Okay, then. So now what?"

"Ah—the other side of you I adore. Totally pragmatic." He chuckled.

"You don't adore me."

"I do, but I admit, I did a terrible job of showing it the last seven weeks."

"Nine weeks."

"No, only seven…count."

She didn't get it. "You might be good at editing, but you're terrible at math."

"No, I'm not. Here's why." He grinned. That damn grin that drove her nuts.

"I'm listening."

"Because the first two weeks you were with me every day."

"How do you know?"

"Because despite being unable to move, despite my eyes refusing to open, despite all of that physical pain, the tubes, the brace, the oxygen, despite all of that, I sensed you. I heard you, Maggie, you crying and praying for me."

"I so did not."

"You so did. I'm glad you did. Don't you get it, Reynolds? You're the reason I'm standing here now."

Maggie wanted to get it. She wanted to believe, to forgive, to move on, to move on *with* Coop. But it was just so damned hard. Asshole Teddy Amato had seen to that. And Ricky. And all the crap in her life. All of it coming together like some big stellar-galactic explosion just to make her life a mound of crap. And she was the only one who could put it all behind her.

Coop kissed her again and did that stupid tucking-her-chin-up-with-one-finger thing, making her feel like a child. He didn't say a word. *What are you waiting for, Coop?* And then it dawned on her.

Nicholas-Nick-Coop-Cooper loved her. He didn't blame her, he wanted her, and she was being so dumb.

"So, you figure it out yet?" His eyes crinkled as he smiled tentatively.

"Yeah. Yes, I think I get it." She took a deep breath, feeling the heaviness in her chest dissipate.

"By George, I think she's got it." His English accent was terrible.

"Oh, great. So besides literary references, now you're into quoting old musicals?"

"Such a smart girl, except it was a play first."

"I know that. George Bernard Shaw."

His grin was sucking her in, making her melt, causing her heart to race. "So, then it's a yes?"

"What's a yes?"

"You'll marry me?" From his pocket he pulled out a small black box. Maggie balked but didn't stop him when he opened the box and slipped the ring on her left index finger.

"It's gigantic."

"Like I said, you're so damned articulate it hurts."

"Okay, here's articulate for you. Why. Would. I. Marry. You. Nick. Coop. Cooper?" She spoke slowly and deliberately, accentuating each word as if to outline the truth.

"Because you love me." His eyes sparkled with something halfway between humor and mischief.

Maggie looked down at the ring. It sparkled brilliantly and was beautiful. Not to mention huge. And she did love him. "Okay, then."

"Okay, then what?" His tone seemed anxious, and he had a question-mark expression on his face.

"Yes. I say yes. I will marry you."

"Matter-of-fact response, but I'll take it." He smiled and kissed her hand. "Oh, by the way. I loved the story. It was a thoughtful Christmas gift."

"That's it?" Maggie said. "Your segue from my 'yes' to your proposal of marriage?" Coop was grinning from ear to ear. "Geeze, talk about Mr. Non-sequitur." Maggie started laughing and replied to his comment. "That was the winning Christmas story. It ended up in the pageant."

"I didn't have to edit it at all."

"Wow. Now I'm worried about whether you're going to be able to work for a living again. Did you hit your head too?"

He didn't answer, and this time, his kiss was much deeper and filled with promise. The pain that they'd both survived, and the losses, sort of floated away into the night sky.

Car horns started honking below in the street; firecrackers were being set off somewhere. Times Square wasn't that far away, and the noise from the crowd was so great they could hear it. Nothing else needed to be said, except they did, in unison: "Happy New Year, sweetheart."

Maggie was lost in the fuzzy, hapless feeling she'd first experienced with her neighbor, Mr. Nick-Coop-Cooper. And the last thing she saw when Coop picked her up and carried her to Liz and Jake's front door was Jake and Liz standing together. Jake handed his wife a crisp bill of unknown denomination, which she accepted with a giant grin and a sort of "I told you so" look on her face.

Maggie whispered in Coop's ear, "She did it."

"Who did what, Reynolds?"

Coop closed the door on the boisterous party, and Maggie answered, "Liz. You and me. Together." She rested her head against his shoulder while fingering the lapel of his tuxedo jacket. "It's pretty amazing if you think about it."

The elevator doors opened. "If you say so, Reynolds." He punched "G" for Garage, and as the doors closed, Coop kissed her.

There was no questioning the care of his embrace—the way he held her, touched her. He was gentle, yet sexy as hell, and she knew Coop would always be that way. No fists. No slice-to-the-bone remarks, just love.

With a sigh against his chest, at last, Maggie let go of the past.

ABOUT THE AUTHOR

Joan traces her roots back to Ireland, England, and Wales. Discounting any inherited pioneer courage, she recently left her home of forty-plus years, and her state of four generations, for the mountains of northern Arizona.

Instead of musing the fates of a hero or heroine along a foggy beach, she now hikes trails looking out to Granite Mountain or the San Francisco Peaks.

Petrified, sure, but she loves her small-town peppered with rodeos, lakes, pines, old trucks, and rocks. Lots of rocks.

The transition made by moving truck instead of covered wagon allowed her to settle into writing full-time.

While support from her four sisters, her children, their spouses, and a crew of grandchildren is a constant, her cowboy-hero husband remains her best bud along with her Labradoodle, Doobie, who practices goofiness, toy-mongering, and provides constructive criticism of character arcs in exchange for walks.

Joan loves hearing from her readers.

X: / AuthorJoanMBird
Facebook: www.facebook.com/joan.m.bird

www.BOROUGHSPUBLISHINGGROUP.com

If you enjoyed this book, please write a review. Our authors appreciate the feedback, and it helps future readers find books they love. We welcome your comments and invite you to send them to info@boroughspublishinggroup.com.

Follow us on TikTok and Instagram, and be sure to sign up for our newsletter for surprises and new releases from your favorite authors.

Are you an aspiring writer? Check out www.boroughspublishinggroup.com/submit and see if we can help you make your dreams come true.

Love podcasts? Enjoy ours at

https://boroughspublishinggroup.com/podcast

www.ingramcontent.com/pod-product-compliance
Lightning Source LLC
Chambersburg PA
CBHW051820170626
46807CB00003B/948